THE
PEARL LAGOON

By

CHARLES NORDHOFF

ILLUSTRATED BY
ANTON OTTO FISCHER

BOSTON
LITTLE, BROWN AND COMPANY

THE ATLANTIC MONTHLY PRESS PUBLICATIONS
ARE PUBLISHED BY
LITTLE, BROWN, AND COMPANY
IN ASSOCIATION WITH
THE ATLANTIC MONTHLY COMPANY

PRINTED IN THE UNITED STATES OF AMERICA

THE PEARL LAGOON

I had my first look at the helmsman.

PREFACE

FOR some months past, my daily stint at the type-writer has been cheered by an ambitious hope: that this story might prove entertaining to the young — the finest of all audiences. They are too wise even to glance at so dull a thing as a preface, but to you older people, who are responsible for what the young ones read, I have a word to say.

I make no claim, in the pages which follow, to have done more than muster the familiar marionettes and put them through their paces before your eyes. In one respect, nevertheless, I venture to commit myself. I know the islands fairly well — white man and native; skipper, trader, and pearl-diver; the sea, the lagoons, the small and lonely bits of land; and I can vouch for the genuineness of the story's atmosphere.

As for the story, there is nothing in it which has not happened, or might not happen to-day — for Romance, like the sea itself, is ever old and ever new.

C. N.

TAHITI, 1924

CONTENTS

I. THE COMING OF THE SCHOONER 3

II. THE PEARLS OF IRIATAI 18

III. ABOARD THE TARA 39

IV. AT FAATEMU 59

V. IRIATAI 75

VI. THE END OF THE SHARK — THE BEGINNING
OF THE DIVING 93

VII. SOUTH SEA FISHERMEN 107

VIII. I TURN PEARL-DIVER 118

IX. THE CAVE OF THE SHARK-GOD 141

X. THE CHOLITA COMES TO IRIATAI 148

XI. PIRACY 173

XII. BOARDERS! 186

XIII. TAHITI 205

ILLUSTRATIONS

I had my first look at the helmsman . . . . . . **Frontispiece**

" You're Charlie, eh ?" he said, when he had looked me up and down with a smile that took me back to the evenings by our fireside, ten years before 12

The shark reared almost vertically beneath the swimmer and opened his great jaws 90

Next moment the wave burst over the gunwale, and we were struggling in the sea 156

THE PEARL LAGOON

O Kahiki, land of the far-reaching ocean,
Land where Olopana dwelt!
Within is the land, outside is the sun!
Indistinct are the sun and the land when approaching.
Perhaps you have seen it?
I have seen it.
I have surely seen Kahiki.

I

THE COMING OF THE SCHOONER

WE lived on the coast of California, on the Spanish grant my grandfather had purchased from the mission which still stands, deserted and crumbling, in the Santa Brigida Valley. Our house, built long before the Civil War, overlooked the lower end of the valley, from a knoll above the salt marshes at the river-mouth. The house was built in the form of a hollow square, surrounding a paved court. The walls were of adobe, — sun-dried bricks of clay, mixed with a little straw, — four feet thick, and pierced by small grated windows, designed for loopholes more than for the admittance of light and air. The beams and rafters were of roughhewn pine, carried down from the mountains by the Santa Brigida Indians, a tribe long since extinct, and the same patient workers had moulded and baked the old red tiles of the roof.

My father and my uncle Harry Selden had been brought up to the half-Spanish life of old California. For ten miles along the coast and six miles inland the land was theirs, and in those days three thousand head of cattle, bearing my grandfather's brand, grazed on the mesas and filed down in long lines to drink. When the brothers were young, the grizzly still lingered in the hills, the tracks of deer and mountain lion were everywhere, the quail trotted in thousands along the river-bottom, and in the winter months the plains along the seacoast were clamorous with flocks of wild geese, feeding on the rich grass. But times were changing, and little by little, civilization was creeping in. A church and a schoolhouse were built in the township north of us; taxes were raised; and finally a party of surveyors appeared, running a line for the new railway. My grandfather abhorred the idea of a railway passing through his land; he made a bitter fight and would not give in till his own lawyer showed him that if he refused to accept what was offered for the right of way, the law would force him to do so for the public good. He died a short time after the trains began to run.

The brothers were young men at that time, and as their mother had been dead for many years, their friends supposed that they would carry on the ranch in a sort of family partnership. But Uncle Harry, in his love of a wild and independent life, was my grandfather over again. He announced that he had had enough of civilization, persuaded my father to buy out his share of the Santa Brigida, and bade his brother and his friends good-bye. I remember, when I was very small, how eagerly we looked forward to the letters my father used to read aloud to us: accounts of African gold-mining; of wanderings in Central America and Mexico; of great cattle-ranches — *estancias*, Uncle Harry called them — in the Argentine; of voyages along the barren Chilean coast;

of storms and shipwrecks among distant archipelagoes. In the end he settled as a trader, a buyer of copra and pearl-shell, in the South Seas.

As for my father, he was content to marry and to stay at home, but he clung to his cattle stubbornly, refusing to farm or to sell an acre of his land and growing poorer with each year that passed. He often said that we would never starve and that our land was constantly increasing in value, but at such times my mother used to rise from her chair with a sigh and walk out alone among her roses in the court. She was a patient woman and she loved my father dearly, but I knew that the sale of only a few acres among all our thousands would have provided her with many things she craved. What with dry years and low prices, our taxes ate up nearly all the profits from the cattle. We could never afford a motor-car or the occasional trips to San Francisco of which our neighbors' children gave me glowing accounts, yet outside of such luxuries, I must own that we had little need of ready money. Our own fat steers provided us and our men with beef; my mother was superintendent of a garden which furnished more vegetables than we could eat; and in the fall and winter game was still plentiful enough to be a real resource.

Our circumstances had made me a rather serious boy, fond of solitude and given to endless daydreams — dreams of returning from vague gold-mines or speculations in land with a fortune, to be invested in the ranch and to provide my mother with travel, and rest, and pretty clothes. On my rides to school along a five-mile stretch of coast, where the pearly fog billowed about the hills and the Pacific broke lazily beyond the dunes, I lived in a world of pure fancy, from which the sight of San Isidro, with its single dusty street, its stores, and hideous frame schoolhouse, recalled me daily with an unpleasant start. All through the week I lived only for the coming Saturday, when I would be free to shoot, or fish in the surf, or ride out with our men to track down some band of half-wild steers, hidden in the thick oak scrub of the foothills.

It was on a Saturday that my uncle came. I was fifteen that winter, and ten years had gone by since he had visited us last, but I had not forgotten his lean powerful figure, or the black eyes lighting up a face tanned to an unfading brown, or the stories he had told a wondering youngster of five, sitting on his knee by the fireplace.

The month was February, as I remember it, for the wild mustard was tall and green on the hills and scattered cock-quail were perched on the fenceposts, filling the air with the long sweet whistle of their mating-time. We were early risers, all of us, and at dawn, as I was eating the breakfast my mother had prepared, she asked me if I would take my gun and try for some wild duck on the marshes. There would be guests from San Isidro to-morrow, and a few brace of duck would be a treat for people from the town. I assented joyfully, for such a request meant that ammunition would be furnished from my father's store, and I loved nothing more than the long lazy hours in a blind, where one could watch the strings of wild fowl trailing across the sky.

I had good sport that morning, hidden close to a shallow pool behind the dunes. As I waded across the marsh, carrying my gun and half-a-dozen wooden decoys, a cloud of teal rose quacking from the grass and headed seaward on beating wings. The redhead were beginning to fly northward from their wintering grounds on the lonely Mexican lagoons; small flocks of them, led by drakes with heads glinting like burnished copper in the sunlight, rose from the creeks ahead of me and sped away, low over the sand hills. At the place that I had chosen for my shooting, I unwound the anchor-lines of the decoys, tossed them far out into the pool, and built myself a rough shelter of pickle-weed, strung on stakes pounded into the mud. I found an old piece of board for a seat, loaded my gun, laid out a box of cartridges within easy reach, and settled myself luxuriously to wait.

Next moment I glanced upward and crouched down lower than before, cocking my old-fashioned hammer-gun. High in the air above the marsh, a flock of sprig was descending in great spiral curves, the wind humming musically through the rigid flight-feathers of their wings. Lower and lower they swung, while my pulse raced as I peeped over the edge of the blind. I could see the snowy breasts of the drakes, the feathers of their long forked tails, and their heads turning this way and that as they scanned the marsh warily for signs of danger. They had seen the decoys, and as they swept past me, still out of range, I called to them, imitating the feeble quack of the hen bird. Then, while I held my breath, they turned again, low over the pool, and came sailing straight at me — necks up and feet dropping to settle among the decoys. My hands were trembling a little, but I took careful aim at the old white-breasted leader, pulled the trigger, and saw him crumple and strike the water with a mighty splash. Wild with alarm, another drake came towering above my head, and leaning backward till I nearly fell off my seat, I let drive with the left barrel and watched him fold his wings and come down plunging to the grass.

I can recall that warm winter morning as if it were yesterday: the steady thunder of the breakers, the perfume of the salt marsh, the wisps of cloud drifting across a soft blue sky. Flock after flock of wild fowl came speeding in from the sea, circled the marsh, set their wings to alight, bounded upward, scattering, at the reports of my gun, and headed back for the ocean — fast-vanishing dots above the dunes. Once a wedge of geese passed at a great height overhead, flying northward with slow steady wing-beats, thrilling me with the hoarse music of their voices. My life seemed cramped and narrow as I gazed at these free rovers of the sky, travelers beyond the far rim of the horizon north and south.

The warm sun and the drowsy chirping and buzzing of insects in the grass brought on a nap that caught me unaware. It must have been mid-day when I awoke with a little start, to sit up and rub my eyes, wondering for an instant where I was. Unloading my gun, I waded out after the decoys and strung my dead birds on a thong of leather. Then, yielding to a habit of those days, I climbed to the top of a sand hill, for a look at the beach. Next moment I nearly shouted aloud in the excitement of what I saw.

Close inshore, not far beyond the outer line of breaking seas, a two-masted schooner was rounding into the wind. She was painted white and her sails shivered crisply in the light air. One needed small knowledge of ships to appreciate the beauty of the little vessel: the high sharp bows, the graceful sweep of sheer, the slender masts, the taut lines of shroud and stay. The sight of a ship was rare along our stretch of coast. At long intervals we saw a trail of smoke far out to sea, — the steamer trading between San Francisco and the west coast of Mexico, — but this was the first time within my memory that a vessel of any kind had passed so close to shore. And she was not merely passing, for I saw now that her crew was sliding a long double-ended boat over the rail. Three men sprang into the whaleboat: a pair of oarsmen who seated themselves and began to pull toward shore, and a man in blue, who stood in the stern, holding a steering-sweep with one hand and waving good-bye to a gigantic figure at the schooner's wheel. The giant raised his hand in an answering wave; the schooner bore off, her sails filled, and she headed out to sea, heeling gracefully to the breeze.

There had been a storm in the north and the swell was high that day. Even from my perch on the dune, the approaching boat was invisible each time it swung down into the trough. It was just beyond the breakers now, and as it rose on the crest of a wave I saw that the oarsmen had ceased to pull and that the man with the steering-sweep had turned his head and was watching the rearing seas astern. The ground swell, as I have said, was very high, rolling shoreward a good ten feet from trough to ridge, and I began to wonder how these three men would win the beach through the turmoil of white water ahead of them. Rearing and tossing as the water shoaled, three or four great waves passed under the boat and crashed forward, racing toward the beach in walls of foam. Then, clear above the thunder of the surf, I heard a vibrant shout — a command in some strange foreign tongue. The men on the seats tugged with a sudden desperate effort at their oars; the man astern, with a single heave of his sweep, turned the boat straight in toward where I lay. He was smoking a cigar, and I felt a thrill of admiration at the easy, careless way he stood at his post. A tremendous comber, with patches of foam beginning to appear along its crest, lifted the boat high in air and swept it forward tilting on the brink of a foaming wall. The wave tumbled and crashed and came rushing far up the beach.

The boat grounded with a gentle shock and the two oarsmen leaped overboard to hold her against the strong backwash. They were brown men, I saw: great brawny fellows more than six feet tall, with handsome, good-natured faces and teeth that flashed when they smiled. The steersman sprang out on the damp sand and gave an order, at which his men dropped a pair of light rollers on the beach and began to drag the boat up beyond highwater mark. Then he came strolling toward the sand hill where I lay hidden in the grass.

He was dressed in blue serge — a double-breasted coat with brass buttons — and a blue yachting-cap with a white crown. His age must have been forty or forty-five, but he was straight as an Indian and carried himself like a boy. His face, of a humorous and rather reckless cast, was tanned almost to the shade of the brown sailors toiling with the boat, and his black eyes were the most brilliant I have ever seen.

His eyes betrayed him. He tossed away the burned-down cigar, folded his arms, and came walking slowly toward my hiding-place, gazing about him with a half-smile on his lips, as if this lonely beach recalled a train of pleasant memories.

I was peering down over a clump of rank salt grass when he glanced up and looked directly into my eyes.

"Uncle Harry!" I shouted as I came sliding and tumbling down the steep face of the dune. His strong hands seized me and lifted me to my feet.

"You're Charlie, eh?" he said, when he had looked me up and down with a smile that took me back to evenings by our fireside, ten years before. "You've done well to remember me all this time! By Jove! I'd never have known you in the world! Here, let's have another look. A chip of the old block, I reckon — you're going to have your grandfather's mouth. Well, I never liked a soft man. How are you all? Did you sight me from the house? Been shooting, eh — let's see your birds."

I led him across the dunes to where I had left my gun and string of duck. At his request I undid the thong about their necks and laid them out on the sand, while he took them up one by one, spreading a wing to admire the changing colors of the speculum, or smoothing the feathers of a glossy head. At last he sighed, as he cut the end of a fresh cigar and looked up at me.

"Ah, Charlie, it takes me back," he remarked. "Many and many a time I've shot over this pond! I had an old muzzle-loader, twice the weight of that gun of yours. On a Friday night your grandfather used to say: 'Which one of you is going

"You're Charlie, eh?" he said, when he had looked me up and down with a smile that took me back to the evenings by our fireside, ten years before.

down to the marsh to-morrow to get me a mess of duck?' and I always landed the job. Your daddy liked to work with the cattle; he reckoned shooting was a chore, like splitting kindling, or driving the milk-cows in from pasture. But it's time for *kaikai*, and I'm keen to see Ben and Mary after all these years. And Marion — she'll be seventeen now, eh? I'll bring my boys up to the house for a bite; the swell was too high to drop anchor, so I told the mate to stand off and on till I came out."

He turned toward the beach and called the sailors in his strong vibrant voice: "*E Ivi! E Ofai e!*" A moment later I saw the two brown men trotting across the dunes. Their feet were bare and they wore sailor jackets and trousers of dungaree. Their round caps bore the schooner's name, Tara, woven in silver thread upon the bands.

"Good lads," remarked my uncle, as they drew near. "Paumotu boys from Rangiroa — they've been with me since the Tara was built. Shake hands with them before we start." He spoke to the sailors in their own tongue, telling them that I was his brother's son, and they smiled as they gazed at me with the frank curiosity of savages. At a word from Uncle Harry, one of them picked up my gun and birds, and I led the way around the marsh to the Santa Brigida road.

We had not walked more than half a mile when we met my father, who had sighted the schooner and was now riding down to the beach.

"Harry!" he exclaimed, his bearded face transformed by an expression I had never seen; and in an instant he was off his horse and wringing my uncle's hand. "It's like you to drop in this way, without an hour's warning, but your welcome will be all the warmer for that! It's good to see you, old fellow! You're looking well — your cannibal islands must agree with you. What do you think of this uncle of yours, eh, Charlie? He wouldn't for the world drop me a wire a day or two ahead, or arrive by train or motor-car, like a civilized man. Nothing will do but to come in a schooner and land like a pirate on the beach! But come along to the house and bring your men; I can't offer them missionary, if that's their usual diet, but we killed a steer yesterday, and there's plenty of fresh beef."

"Well, Ben," said Uncle Harry, still clasping my father's hand, "ten years haven't changed you, after all! I can't tell you how good it is to be back on the Santa Brigida again! Your boy says that Mary and Marion are well — come, I want to see them; let's be getting along. I'll bring my sailors, if I may. No need to ask how you are — rugged as an old grizzly, eh?"

At sight of Uncle Harry my mother forgot her cares, and only the joy of preparing dinner for him persuaded my sister Marion to leave his side. We dined at midday in the old-fashioned manner, and that afternoon we lingered long at table, until a whispering buzz of talk from the courtyard told

us that the news had spread — that my grandfather's old retainers were assembling to greet the
boy they had known so many years before. Motion-
ing us to keep our places, Uncle Harry rose from
his chair with a smile and walked out through the
door to the sunny court beyond.

I heard a chorus of exclamations in Spanish:
"Don Enrique! Patroncito! Ay, Dios Mio!" and
the voice of old Juana, the white-haired woman
who had nursed him as a child, sobbing aloud as
she murmured over and over: "My child, my
child — you have not forgotten old Juana, no?"
He had an almost uncanny faculty for winning
people's love.

We sat late that evening about the fire of oak
logs in the living-room. Even to-day the scent of
wood smoke brings back the picture of that long,
dim-lit room, with its ceiling, so lofty that parts
of it were lost in shadow, crossed by great roughhewn beams, blackened by half a century of smoke.
The heads of antelope and deer and bighorn looked
down from the walls, and close to the chimney my
grandfather's silver-mounted spurs and old Sharp's
rifle hung from a peg. The floor was covered with
the skins of animals that he had shot: wildcat
and mountain lion; grizzlies from San Gorgonio
and Temescal; a moth-eaten buffalo-robe from
the days when he had crossed the plains.

At last we rose to bid my mother and Marion
good-night. Eager to hear what my uncle would
have to say, I seated myself inconspicuously in a

high-backed chair, and at that moment my father turned and noticed me. "Bedtime, Charlie," he said in his firm, kindly way. But Uncle Harry was of a different mind.

"Let him sit up for once," he put in, with a twinkle in his dark eyes; "I want to have a yarn with you, and I want Charlie to hear what I have to say. Don't complain if I keep you up the best part of the night, for this is my only chance. I am going to tell you a story, which will explain why I must leave to-morrow, and why I ask you to let Charlie go with me when I sail."

"Sailing to-morrow!" exclaimed my father, sitting up suddenly in his chair; "and you want to take Charlie away! That's a deuce of a thing to tell me the first time I've seen you for ten years! Why in the world must you rush away so fast?"

My uncle smiled a wry smile.

"It's hard to leave so soon," he said. "I wish I could spend a month or two with you, wandering over the old place and having a bit of sport. But I'm short of time. I've been in San Francisco, having a motor installed in the Tara, and the people at the shipyard were slow. I would have communicated with you, but I did n't want to make any rash promises, and it began to look as if I would n't have time to put in here at all. I'll be up next year for a real visit — on my word; but to-morrow I must sail; I'm going to take Charlie with me if I have to sit up all night persuading you."

Uncle Harry gave me one of his brilliant glances,

tempered with a wink, and I felt my heart beat with excitement at the prospect opening suddenly before me. He rose to his feet, took a pair of long thin cigars from his case, offered one to my father, and sank back into his chair, cocking his heels high against the rough stone of the fireplace.

"Now," he went on, blowing a cloud of smoke toward the ceiling, "if you're not too sleepy, I'm going to tell you how I came to hear of the pearls in Iriatai Lagoon."

II

THE PEARLS OF IRIATAI

"IRIATAI," my uncle began, "is an atoll in the Paumotus — a narrow ring of land nowhere more than a few yards high, surrounding a lagoon ten or twelve miles across. The island has a curious history, for its people were the last to remain savages among all the eighty islands of the group. It is a lonely place, far out to the eastward where trading-schooners seldom pass, and long after the missionaries had civilized the other atolls, Iriatai remained unknown — no white man had landed on its beaches, or laid eyes on the wild people whose village was screened by the dense bush along the shore.

"In those days there was a famous Catholic school on Mangareva in the Gambier group, and one year, at Christmas time, a brig set sail from Tahiti for the South, with a cargo of trade, and half a dozen children of wealthy half-caste families, sent to be educated by the Church. A week after the brig's departure, a gale came roaring down out of the northwest — a storm so fierce and long-continued that old men speak of it to this day. On Tahiti there was great anxiety for the vessel's safety, and no one was surprised when many months later a schooner came north from Mangareva, with word that the brig had never arrived. It was an old story, — another ship lost somewhere in the lonely spaces of the South Pacific, — but there was one woman on Tahiti who refused to believe that the vessel was lost. She was a rich widow whose only child, a flaxen-haired girl of eight, was missing with the others, and she offered great rewards to anyone who could bring her news of the ship.

"One day a trading skipper came to her with a clew. On his last trip through the Paumotus he had been blown far out of his course, and while hove-to in a heavy sea, he had raised an island only vaguely marked on the charts. He ran in to take shelter in the lee, and as they stood off and on, close to the leeward reef, the lookout had reported people ashore. Taking up his glass, the captain made out a crowd of savages standing on the beach. They brandished spears and were dressed in girdles of pandanus leaf, but two or three of them wore about their shoulders pieces of cloth which the skipper took to be of European make. He was an old-timer in the islands, and he was certain that no trader had ever visited the place.

"The widow lost no time in fitting up an expedition at her own expense. The skipper who had seen the savages on Iriatai was given command; the old man is living in Papeete to-day — I had the yarn from him. He picked up half a dozen Rangiroa boys and armed them with rifles in case of trouble, though they were instructed not to shoot unless attacked.

"After a fortnight of beating about, they raised

the palms of Iriatai, sailed in through the pass, dropped anchor a stone's throw off the village, and went ashore. There were canoes hauled up on the beach, fishing tackle lay about as it had been dropped in haste, and the thatched huts seemed to have been inhabitated within an hour past, but saving a dog or two and a few half-wild pigs, no living creature was in sight. The captain heard a shout from one of his men who was exploring the far end of the village, and the others hastened to the place where the Christian boy was pointing with horror to the ground. There, close to the temple of the islanders, — a long platform of rude coral blocks, — was the *umu tagata:* the oven in which human bodies were roasted whole. The bones of men, clean-picked by the cannibals of Iriatai, were scattered on all sides, and hundreds of Chilian silver dollars — current throughout the Pacific in those days — were arranged in neat patterns about the cooking-place. A few yards off, mounted on sharpened stakes along the coral wall, a row of heads was drying in the sun, and one of them — a small head from which hung wisps of long flaxen hair — made the whole story clear. The widow's daughter had been found.

"The skipper was sickened — if he had caught the people then, he told me, he would have slaughtered them like sheep. Calling to his men, he set off recklessly through the bush, resolved to shoot down the savages at sight. Hour after hour the searchers struggled through the dense green bush, scratched by thorns, streaming with perspiration, stumbling over the sharp coral underfoot. It was a hot still day, and the jungle was lifeless and strangely quiet. No leaf stirred, no bird sang, and the drooping fronds of palms hung motionless overhead. Nothing moved anywhere saving the small white sea-birds which circled eerily, high above the tree-tops. The oppression of the bush cooled the skipper's anger and lowered the spirits of the searching-party; no word had been spoken for half an hour when they sat down in silence to rest, close to a pile of jagged coral blocks. Leaning against a tree-trunk, with his rifle between his knees, the captain was in the act of filling a pipe when one of the men touched his arm, signing him to make no sound. To one side of them, in the bleached mass of coral, there was a faint scratching noise, and presently, as they watched, a brown hand and arm appeared for an instant in a crevice of the rocks.

" 'That is their hiding-place,' the native breathed into the skipper's ear; 'I have heard my own people speak of such caverns, where they took refuge in the old wars.'

"The captain thought for a moment before he spoke. 'Go alone to the mouth of the cave,' he whispered to the boy beside him; 'our rifles will protect you. See if you can talk to the savages, and if they understand you, try to persuade one or two of the men to come out.'

"The native rose and stole away, and soon they

heard his voice calling softly in the Paumotan tongue. He seemed to be in conversation with the people underground. When he returned there was an odd smile on his lips. 'It is strange,' he said, 'those people speak a tongue such as our old men use. They are like beasts or cruel children, killing because they know no better, or are afraid. I do not believe that they are evil men. There is no entrance to the cave — only a little hole in the rock, through which a man may thrust his hand and arm. The place is sacred in these people's eyes and on the ground close to the hole there is an offering of food. They feared it might betray their hiding-place; the man we saw was trying to reach it from within. There is another way out, they said, knowing that I could never find the place. To reach it, they swim beneath the water of the lagoon. We cannot get in from above; all our strength would not suffice to move the rocks. They are afraid to come out, but perhaps I might persuade them if I could show gifts such as they have never seen.'

"The captain collected a few bright trifles among his men: a mirror or two, a gaudy bandanna handkerchief, a clasp knife with a glittering blade. The native returned to parley with the savages, and while he was gone the skipper gave instructions to his men — they were to scatter a little and lie hidden; if the wild people found courage to leave their cave, and they were not too many, they were to be seized and bound at once.

"An hour passed. Then, without the warning crackle of a twig, two savages stepped from the bush and came toward the native who awaited them, holding out gifts and speaking encouragingly. They were naked save for light girdles of grass, and their shocks of hair were tied in high knots upon their heads. The captain whistled, and a moment later the two men of Iriatai lay triced and helpless on the ground.

"The schooner sailed for Tahiti the same night, carrying the prisoners, whose evidence — the story, freely told, of how the wrecked brig had been plundered before she broke up, and how every soul aboard had been massacred — was placed before the French authorities. A few months later a man-of-war was sent to Iriatai, with one of the prisoners as interpreter, and the people of the island were carried off to Tahiti to be civilized. In the end, the chief was executed in reprisal for the island's crime, and his people were taken away to distant atolls of the group.

"Only one of them, so far as I know, ever returned to Iriatai — Turia, the chief's daughter, a girl of eleven or twelve when she was carried off aboard the man-of-war. Her beauty and intelligence attracted the notice of a half-caste Tahitian, who adopted her and gave her an education at the Sisters' School. At seventeen she married the Baron von Tesmar — an Austrian nobleman, a man of wealth and taste, brought up among the capitals of the Old World. He was well known in all the outlandish ports of the Pacific; for reasons of his own, of which he never spoke, he had chosen to shut the door on the past. He traveled on his own yacht with a Kanaka crew, and during a visit to Tahiti he ran across Turia, the girl from Iriatai. A month later she sailed away with him, with a marriage certificate, all legal and shipshape, stowed away in her camphorwood box. I suppose she must have been the Baroness von Tesmar — By Jove, a funny world!

"The natives have a quality I like: each one of them loves his own island in a way that we can scarcely understand. Turia was no exception, but unlike the rest of her people, she ended her days on Iriatai. A short time after he married her the Baron became interested in pearl-culture and — at her suggestion, no doubt — they settled on the island where her savage forefathers had lived and died.

"To give you an understanding of the story from now on, I must tell you one or two things about pearl-shell, which furnishes the mother-of-pearl used all over the world for buttons and ornaments and the handles of knives. In the Paumotus where I trade, the pearl-oysters are of a kind called 'black-lipped,' valuable as mother-of-pearl but rather barren so far as real pearls are concerned. Out to the west, about Celebes and in the Sulu Sea, there is another variety, richer in pearls and far more valuable as shell, called 'gold-lipped,' because the edges of the shell are golden-tinted.

Von Tesmar was a man of some scientific attainments, and he suspected, far ahead of his time, that the growth of a pearl in the oyster was caused by a parasite, which it might be possible to transmit by artificial means. In order to carry out his experiments, he had his schooner fitted with a kind of well, through which the sea water was allowed to circulate, and brought shipments of live oysters from distant parts, to be transplanted in Iriatai Lagoon. He may have had an idea that the gold-lipped oysters, in this new environment, would prove more susceptible to infection — to the little-known parasite believed to cause the pearl.

"The Baron's career, his studies of the pearl, and his new settlement on Iriatai were all ended by the hurricane of 1881. The island had been one of the finest of the Paumotus, with dense groves of coconuts and a deep soil on the higher spots, but when I first landed there, in ninety-six, it was a waste of sand and tumbled coral-blocks, clean-swept from end to end by breaching seas. On an islet, far down the lagoon, a small clump of palms remained — the only living things, save Turia and her child, to survive the fury of the sea.

"The settlement was at the weather end, and when the seas began to breach across into the lagoon, von Tesmar's schooner was anchored fifty yards offshore. Both cables snapped and she disappeared in an instant among the driving clouds downwind. She must have piled up at the leeward end, or perhaps she was carried clean over into the open sea beyond. At any rate, no man of her crew was ever seen again. The people of the settlement — a dozen natives with their wives, brought by von Tesmar to labor in the oyster-beds — had no time to chop off the tops of the palms in which they took refuge. A pair of old palms, eighty feet high, flexible and tough as whalebone, stood close beside the house. High up on the bole of one, the Baron tied himself, and Turia swarmed up the other, her three-year-old boy lashed to her back.

"It is useless to try to describe a South Sea hurricane. One after another, the houses were carried away. Each frothing comber seemed to rush over the land more fiercely than the last; the wind came in gusts that bent the palms like reeds. With a sound audible above the uproar of the hurricane, a palm-bole snapped, and its top, with two human beings clinging among the fronds, sped off to vanish in the wrack. Turia's was the last to withstand the wind; she watched the others go, — men, women, and babies at their mothers' breasts, — and finally a faint, splitting report close by told her that von Tesmar's palm had given way. Next moment her own refuge went, and still clinging to the upper bole, she was sailing above the torn white surface of the lagoon. How she survived the impact, disentangled herself from the wreckage, and lived through miles of angry water is a thing that I have never understood. When she struggled ashore on the islet which was the only land above the sea, her child was still alive. No one but a Paumotan could have done it, and no woman of any other race could have lived and supported her child — as Turia did for many weeks — on coconuts and the fish she was able to catch with her bare hands. In the end, the lookout of a passing schooner saw her signal-smoke."

My uncle's cigar had gone out and he rose for a moment to scratch a match against the fireplace. The lamp was turned low; the glowing logs on the andirons sent waves of light flickering among the shadows of the room. My father stood up to stretch his legs. Standing with hands clasped behind his back, he gazed quizzically at his brother, seated in the deep old leather chair.

"That's a good story of yours, as far as it goes," he observed; "but what has all this to do with you, or with the fact that you can spend only one day with us?"

"No wonder you're growing impatient," said Uncle Harry, with a smile; "it must seem an interminable yarn, but it's all linked together, as you will see. I came into it about ten years ago, when I took a lease on Iriatai. It was just after my last visit here. A friend suggested that I have a look at the island with a view to planting coconuts — they thrive wonderfully in the coral of the atolls. I had heard half-legendary accounts of von Tesmar and his pearls, but such experiments are not taken seriously in the islands, where so many cranks have tried this scheme or that, and failed. The lagoon had never been a place for shell.

"I met Turia when I landed there. Von Tesmar had left her a little money in the Papeete bank, and after a year of civilization, she had been over-powered by the homing instinct of her race. Her husband had relatives in German Samoa — the directors of a great Apia trading-house — and she took her child to them before she set out to end her days on Iriatai. Then she chartered a small schooner and sailed away with a couple of poor native families and a stock of provisions and seed-coconuts. I found her happy in a lonely sort of life, settled in a one-room cottage, surrounded by groves of fine twelve-year-old palms. The place was furnished with a bed, an accordion, and a chest of camphorwood; a portrait of von Tesmar, in the uniform of an officer of dragoons, hung on the wall. There must have been a human side of this man's character, for his widow remembered him with a devotion hard to match.

"She was the only claimant to rights in the island, and I had no difficulty in gaining her consent. Within a year I obtained from the French Government a long lease on Iriatai and now there are sixty thousand young palms on the island, some of them already beginning to bear. Another hurricane? We can't afford to think of that — they strike an island not more than once in every hundred years. During the visits when I carried labor and supplies to Iriatai, Turia used to spin me yarns about the hurricane. She was an inter-

esting woman, as those of the pure old blood are
apt to be. When I knew her she was straight and
handsome still — no darker than a woman of
southern Spain. Sometimes she showed me letters
from her boy, growing up in far-off Samoa with
his relatives. I did not meet him till after she was
dead.

"I needed a rest last year, and as I did n't have
time for a run up to see you all, I decided to take
a vacation among the islands — a short cruise
through the Tongan and Samoan groups. One
night in Apia, the German port, I had been dining
at the consulate, and as I walked along the moonlit
beach to where my boat's crew awaited me, I was
stopped by a young half-caste, dressed in soiled
white duck. He spoke English, and he looked so
miserable, so poor and ill that it needed a thicker
skin than mine to pass him without a word. His
body was no more than skin and bones, and when
he turned in the moonlight, I saw the wreck of
what had been a handsome face, ravaged by quick
tropical tuberculosis. He spoke in abrupt sentences,
gasping for breath and stopping at intervals to
cough.

" 'You English?' he asked. 'No? American,
eh? I speak German, French — not much English.
That Tara your schooner? They tell me you go
Tahiti to-morrow. Give me passage, eh? I cook
— wash dishes — cabin boy — anything! I want
go Tahiti too much!'

"He turned away from me and leaned over with

a hand to his chest, coughing frightfully; when the paroxysm had passed he stood gasping and unable to speak. It was impossible not to be sorry for the poor devil.

"'I'll let you know to-morrow,' I told him. 'I'm sailing at sundown. Come to the beach at four or five o'clock.'

"Next morning, strolling with the American consul, I pointed out the half-caste, asleep in the shade of a beached canoe. 'Oh, that fellow,' said the consul; 'Yes, I know him; von Tesmar's his name. Does n't look much like a nobleman, does he? As a matter of fact, he's a baron of the Austrian Empire — when he's drunk enough he'll show you the papers to prove it! Odd story. His father married a Paumotu woman years ago and was lost in a hurricane, back in the eighties. The mother brought her child out here — old Madame Lichtenstein, of the Hamburg Concession, was the youngster's aunt. The old lady was good to him, sent him to the Protestant school and finally shipped him off to Europe with plenty of money to spend. But the cold winters were too much for his native blood, I guess; t. b. got him after the second year, and as happens so often in the islands, consumption led to drink. Then one day he turned up here, a yellow skeleton with a craving for alcohol. The Germans took pity on him and pensioned him off for a time, but he was sinking rather low, and finally they cut off the money and ceased to recognize him at all. One can't really blame them much!'

"I did n't say anything, but I was interested, I'll admit. So this was Turia's son — the child of the hurricane on Iriatai! He had traveled a long road since those days; but I suspected that the end was near. Why should he want to go to the eastern islands? The old instinct of his mother's blood, perhaps, calling the wanderer home at last to die.

"I gave him a passage, at any rate. He was willing enough, but it was absurd to talk of working his way — when we'd been out three days I knew that his eyes would never see another landfall. I put him in a berth in the spare stateroom. He'd picked up his English on the beach, but in French you'd have been surprised to hear the fellow talk. With the interest one cannot help feeling in a dying man, I spent a good deal of time yarning with him, and finally told him that I had heard something of his story and had known Turia on Iriatai. He was in a steady low fever by this time, and our talks seemed to excite him; he asked endless questions about his mother and her life — the island — the lagoon.

"One night, when I was at the wheel, the cabin boy came on deck, rubbing the sleep from his eyes, to say that von Tesmar wanted to see me at once. There was something of great importance to tell me, it seemed. We were in the middle of the wide, lonely reach of sea that stretches from Rose Island to the Leeward group. The moon had risen about eleven o'clock; there was not a cloud in the sky, and a steady breeze blew warm and fair from the

northwest. I had taken the wheel at moonrise
and I hated to go below, but the half-caste's message seemed so urgent that I called the man on
watch to take my place.

"I found von Tesmar gasping in his berth. He
had gotten up to undo a bundle he carried with
him, wrapped in a piece of native cloth, and when
I pulled the curtain aside, he held out to me a
tattered sheet of cheap ruled notepaper.

"'For you,' he whispered breathlessly, in the
French he had picked up during an edifying year
in Paris. 'Ah, *mon ami*, this is the end — now I
must die, and a glass of your excellent rum would
help me to die gracefully. *Merci bien* — you are
kindness personified! I wonder why: there is so
little, in your eyes, that I can do. Yes, this is the
end. I cannot complain — I have had my fun
and paid for some of it, at least. Never again shall
I watch the faces passing my table on the boule-
vard, nor sit with the brown people in a bush-
clearing far from the church, while the drums
throb and the sleek young girls twist and flutter
their hands in the torchlight. No doubt you are
thinking that I am a *drôle de type*, and so I am, by
training and by birth — half savage, half *boule-
vardier*. But the time is short and I weary you
with idle reflections; *allons*, to business! You can
read the native Tahitian, eh? It is difficult for one
who knows only the Samoan dialect. I had hoped
to keep that paper to myself; the doctors say that
men with my malady are always optimists. But

you have treated me as one white man treats another — keep it, read it, and do as you please. Perhaps it is worth another glass of rum, *n'est-ce pas?* Another rum for Monsieur le Baron! They called me that in Paris, at the Grand Hotel — Ha, ha! Noble on both sides, *bon Dieu!* — my mother a cannibal Princess — Monsieur le Baron von Tesmar, Prince of Iriatai! How's that for a title, *hein?*'

"At five o'clock, when the moonlight paled before the first flush of dawn, he turned his face away from me and died. I blew out the light and went on deck to give orders for his burial. Then, when I had my coffee, I lay down in my berth and unfolded the paper he had given me. It proved a quaint document — a letter in the native language from Turia to her son, written a few days before her death. Here it is — it is worth translating for your benefit: —

This from your dear mother, who loves you and prays that God's blessing may bring you prosperity and health. *Amen.* I am ill, and though the woman who tends me has made medicine, I think that I shall soon die. Do not weep for me — I shall be happy to be again with your father, whom I have always loved. Now pay attention, for there is a thing that I must tell you. Your father was a wise man, and his work was to bring pearl oysters from foreign seas to this lagoon. After the hurricane, when I swam so far with you clinging to my back, I believed for many years that the oysters must all be dead, but that was not true. In the far end of the lagoon, where no one goes to-day, I have found where the strange shells with edges like gold lie on the coral in thousands, not more than fifteen fathoms deep. Many times I have gone alone in my canoe to dive for them, and I have found fine pearls, great and small. These are true words. The white man called Seroni, who brings people to plant coconuts on Iriatai, is a good man and my friend, but I have said nothing of the pearls to him. They were your father's work, and you will want them, since you live in the white man's land. The oysters are on coral bottom, midway between the islet and the reef. Beware of a great brown shark when you come here to dive; he comes sometimes to that end of the lagoon, and twice he has nearly had me when I was intent upon my work. I think he is the old god of my people, worshiped when I was a child. Farewell, my dear son — I shall not see you again.

On Iriatai, from Turia, to her son, Arno von Tesmar

"Somehow, as I read this letter, I was convinced that what the woman said was true. There are nearly a hundred square miles in Iriatai Lagoon, and though my men did a good deal of fishing, a shell-patch of the largest size might have escaped their notice for years. No one in the Eastern Pacific had ever succeeded in acclimatizing the gold-lipped shell, but that did not prove that it could not be done. If Turia's words were true, von Tesmar's eagerness to reach the group was justified. It might prove a rare chance, and I resolved to investigate at once.

"Fatu, my big mate, is a man that I can always trust. He is a first-class diver, and when the Tara was anchored at Iriatai, I told him the story and explained that he must hold his tongue. We took a big canoe and made camp on the islet at the far end of the lagoon. Even with Turia's directions, it took us four days to find the shell, but when

Fatu began to bring up the gold-lipped oysters in both hands, I saw that the dead half-caste had paid his passage a thousandfold.

My man reported the bottom covered with shell for acres on either side—a little fortune in mother-of-pearl alone. And pearls — By Jove, I could scarcely drag Fatu away!

"I did n't dare to linger — there was danger of causing talk. It would need a dozen or fifteen divers to work the patch properly; the news would travel like a whirlwind, and I had n't the shadow of a claim on the shell. The open lagoons — I must explain — with passes through which a vessel can enter from the sea are Government property, and during the legal season any native may dive and keep what he obtains. Unless I did some careful planning, half the schooners in the South Pacific would soon be anchored at Iriatai. Well, I headed for Tahiti and did my thinking on the way. The Governor of French Oceania is a friend of mine. When we reached Papeete my plans were made and I put the matter up to his common-sense: By pure chance, in one of the atolls under his administration I had discovered a brand-new patch of shell. (I said nothing, of course, about von Tesmar, or the fact that the shell was golden-lipped.) If properly preserved and worked, this patch might in the future prove a valuable asset to the Government. As things were, I could not legally profit by my discovery — any Kanaka diver had as much right as I to exploit the new lagoon. If I

held my tongue, a hundred years might pass before
another man stumbled on the place. In view of all
this, therefore, would n't it be fair to give me one
season's exclusive rights, in return for adding a
new pearl-lagoon to the five or six already under
French control?

"It struck me as a fair thing to ask, and I had
little difficulty with the Governor. Within a month
the papers were delivered to me all signed and
sealed: a year's rights to the shell and pearls of
Iriatai. I had always wanted an engine for the
Tara and now I felt that I could afford one. In
the Paumotus, with reefs and five-knot currents
and frequent calms, a motor is better than a dozen
insurance policies. Now the engine's installed and
I am heading back without a day to waste. It will
take time to find the men, to build canoes, and
get the diving under way."

As he finished his story, my uncle rose and began
to pace back and forth before the fireplace. My
father lay in his chair, smoking and making no
comment; I fancy that the glimpse of an adventurous life on the other side of the world had set his
thoughts to wandering. Though it was long past
midnight, I was wide awake.

All at once my uncle stopped beside his brother's
chair and stood looking down at him, with a half-
apologetic smile.

"See here, Ben," he said, "I want you to let
Charlie come along. A few months out of school

will do no harm and I'll give you my word to have
him back in the fall. I've come to the age when a
man feels the need of youngsters, and yours are all
I have. There'll be plenty of work — I need some-
one I can really trust. He'll have his share in what
we get, of course, and he'll earn it — I'll see to
that. Be a good fellow, and let him come!"

My father looked up and sighed before he spoke.
"Ah, Harry," he remarked, "you're a lucky man!
All your life you've been a rainbow-chaser and
now you seem to have caught up with one at last.
It's hard not to envy you when I hear a story like
the one you've told! I didn't realize what a dull
old stay-at-home I had become. As for the boy,
I'm tempted to let him go; but you're asking a
good deal! You live in a rough part of the world,
if the stories one hears are true. There must be
men down there who would make it hot for you
if the news of your pearl-lagoon leaked out. Even
in California we used to hear of the exploits of
Bully Hayes."

My uncle smiled and shook his head.

"Those days are past," he said. "Pease and
Hayes are dead, and they've left no successors in
the Eastern Pacific. So far as I know, there's
only one scoundrel of that type left in Polynesia
and he operates far out to the west: 'Thursday
Island Schmidt' — ever hear of him? I don't
know him myself, and I'm not hankering to make
his acquaintance until this job is done. But he's
never been east of Samoa, and even old Thursday

Island would hesitate to tackle a barefaced hold-up nowadays. Warships and the wireless have ended all that. Let the boy come — I'd be the last man to drag him into any scrapes."

"He can go, then," said my father, rising from his chair. "I only wish I'd had such a chance when I was a youngster. But you'll have to talk his mother around — I wash my hands of that! We'll leave that for tomorrow, eh? Come, you must be tired; we'd better turn in, all three of us."

And so the matter was left, while I wandered in a daze to my room and lay down to spend a night made sleepless by mingled anxiety and happiness.

III

ABOARD THE TARA

It must have taken a deal of talking to win my
mother's consent, but Uncle Harry proved equal to
the task. When we had breakfasted he sat with
her for an hour in the courtyard, and afterward,
when I saw her alone, she kissed me and told me
that I was to go.

We had guests that day — old friends who had
known my uncle when he was a boy. I sat at dinner with the others, but all I can remember of the
meal is that Uncle Harry praised my ducks. I was
still dazed at my good fortune: my dreams of adventure and of distant wanderings were to come
true at last! A cruise on the Tara in the South
Seas — a quest for pearls in a tropical lagoon —
a part in the sequel of my uncle's tale — indeed,
the prospect was enough to intoxicate any boy of
fifteen. Iriatai! There was magic in the word
alone, and I repeated it under my breath while
the older people about me spoke of commonplace
things.

The sun was low over the Pacific when we said
good-bye. The others accompanied us to the beach:
my father and mother, Marion, and our guests;
and in a little group of people from the Santa
Brigida I saw old Juana sobbing, with a shawl
pulled over her head. The two sailors rolled the

whaleboat into the wash of the sea; after the final handclasps, Uncle Harry and I took our places in the stern. The ocean was calmer than on the day before. Ivi and Ofai watched their time, ran the boat out in a lull, leaped in to seize their oars, and pulled seaward through the gentle surf. The mate of the Tara had seen us with his glasses and the schooner was headed toward the land. Presently we came alongside, scrambled over the rail, and helped the sailors haul the boat on deck. My uncle shouted a command; the sheets were slacked away, and the Tara bore off to the southwest.

I turned for a last look at the watchers on the beach, already so far distant that they were no more than a patch of color against the dunes. There was a lump in my throat — it was the first time that I had been away from home.

"I hate to leave," remarked Uncle Harry, who was standing at my side, "but we're off now; in the morning we'll be out of sight of land. Come below and have a look at your quarters. I think you'll like the Tara; she's my only child!"

The Tara, as I have said, was schooner-rigged — a vessel of a hundred tons, fast, comfortable, and designed to ride out any sea. A glance convinced me of her owner's love. The sides were snowy with fresh paint; the decks of white pine were holystoned till they gleamed spotless against their seams of pitch; the masts and spars were newly varnished, and no spot of mildew stained the sails. On the after deck a shallow cockpit contained the

wheel and binnacle. Forward of the cockpit, the
companionway led down to the saloon, where a
pair of curtained doors gave on staterooms to starboard and to port. The woodwork was of bright
mahogany. On either side of the saloon there was
a leather-upholstered lounge, and half a dozen
chairs were screwed fast to the floor about a handsome dining-table. Forward of the saloon was the
engine-room, shut off by a bulkhead from the
main hold where burlapped bales and packing-
cases were piled high between decks. The galley
was on deck, and the forecastle was placed far up
in the bows, furnished with a deal-table and berths
made of piping on which lengths of heavy canvas
had been stretched.

My uncle's was the larger of the two staterooms.
It was fitted with a washstand and a single berth;
a few framed photographs hung on the walls, a
large porthole gave a view of the sea outside, and
a steel safe was built into one corner of the room.
The cabin opposite was assigned to me — it was
here that the half-caste son of von Tesmar had
breathed his last.

"You're not afraid of ghosts, eh?" my uncle
asked me with a smile. "The poor devil died in
that very bunk, but he's never troubled us since,
and if he did appear, he'd be harmless enough.
Come — I want you to know my boys; excepting
the cook I shipped in 'Frisco, I've known them all
for years."

They were Kanakas — brown Polynesians of the

islands, akin to the Hawaiian people and to the
Maoris of far-away New Zealand. Ivi and Ofai I
already knew. Fatu, the mate, was a huge silent
fellow with a smile in his quick dark eyes — a
nobly proportioned giant. The engineer, Pahuri,
was an elderly Rarotongan with a passion for fishing: a small man, gray, wrinkled, and talkative.
He had followed the sea since boyhood and had
visited many parts of the world on whaling vessels
and on merchant ships. His heart was kind, but he
possessed a biting tongue and his travels had made
him cynical. Then came Rairi, the half-caste cook
my uncle had found stranded in San Francisco
after a voyage before the mast. He was a shade
lighter than the others, with a handsome, sullen
face: a tall man and powerfully built, though
dwarfed in the presence of the mate. Rairi spoke
a little English, picked up along the waterfront,
and had a pleasant manner when he wished to make
himself agreeable, but at other times his features
were of a forbidding cast. He cooked, and cooked
well, in his box of a galley, set on the forward deck
above the hold. Outside of his duties he had little
to do with the men, as if his strain of white blood
caused him to hold aloof. Last of all came Marama
the cabin boy, who served our meals, polished
brasses, and made himself useful whenever there
was an odd job on hand. He was a brown lad of
my own age, though larger and much stronger
than I, and I liked him from the moment we met.
He was a cheerful worker, his black eyes were

bright with humor and intelligence, and he never
lost his temper when a lurch of the deck threw a
potful of hot coffee over his feet. His father, Uncle
Harry told me, was a chief on Raiatea.

"We're heading straight for Raiatea," said my
uncle as we sat at dinner that night. "I want you
to stop there while I run across to unload my cargo
at Tahiti. It's a fine island and the chief of Faatemu is a great friend of mine. You can put up at
his house; I'll leave young Marama to keep you
company. He knows a bit of English — that will
help you at first. By the way, you'll need to pick
up the native as fast as you can; the man who
can't speak with them is handicapped. It's easy to
learn; why not work at it during our passage
South? I'll help you and so will any of the men;
it always pleases them to find one of us interested
in their language. Try memorizing a few words
a day at the start, then the simple phrases will
come to you, and before you know it, you'll be
yarning with the crew.

"The quieter we keep this business the less
trouble we'll have, and for that reason I'm going
to pick up my men on Raiatea. There's a Paumotan colony on the island — we'll have no trouble in
getting all the divers we need. They work two in
a canoe, and we'll want fifteen canoes to be on the
safe side. They'll have to be built specially; I want
you to stay in Faatemu to see that they are ready
when I return. It's a great place for fishing and
pig-hunting — you'll have a lot of fun!"

When dinner was over we sat on deck for a time, while my uncle smoked one of his slender black cigars. The sails were furled, for the wind had died away an hour after sunset. An oily swell was running from the west and the pulsing of the Tara's engine drove us steadily away from land. By the dim light of the binnacle I could see that Ofai, at the wheel, was shivering. Finally he called to Ivi, and the other came aft with a thick woollen jacket on his arm. Uncle Harry tossed the stump of his cigar overboard; I heard it hiss for an instant as it struck the sea.

"Come," he said; "let's turn in before we're both frozen. My blood's too thin for these chilly winters of yours!"

Next day we left the zone of coastwise calms and ran into the northeast trade. The engine was stopped and the Tara headed southward with all sails set, running almost free. It is a brave wind, the trade, and it blew strong and fair, making the whitecaps dance on the dark blue swells, and driving us southward day after day till we were within a few degrees of the Line. Each day, at noon, my uncle fetched his sextant on deck to observe the sun, and I watched him afterward, bending over the chart in his stateroom, marking off our position with dividers and scale. Finally, with a very sharp pencil, he made a tiny cross, and I knew that this mark on the great blank spaces of the mid-Pacific was where the schooner had been at twelve o'clock.

Sometimes the wind fell away at sunset and the

engine chugged steadily throughout the night;
once, when the trade blew day and night without
abating, the Tara reeled off two hundred knots
from noon to noon.

The weather grew warmer day by day. Shoes,
stockings, and warm clothing were stowed away,
and the men went about their work in waistcloths,
with brown chests bare. One morning Uncle Harry
called me into the trade-room at the after end of
the hold, and handed me half a dozen *pareus* —
strips of cotton print, dyed in barbaric patterns of
scarlet and white, a yard wide and two yards long.

"If I were you," he said, "I'd put away my
trousers from now on — shirts too, if you're not
afraid of the sun. My friends call me a savage,
but aboard my own schooner I dress as I please.
The natives invented the pareu, and it's the most
sensible dress for this part of the world. It's cooler
than pyjamas at night, and in the morning you
have merely to hitch a fresh one around your
waist and you're dressed for the day. Let me show
you the trick of putting it on." He wrapped the
cloth about my waist, tucked in the ends and
made a tight roll at the top. "There," he remarked
with a smile, "that's quick dressing, eh?"

From that day we went barefoot and bare-
chested as the sailors did, and I was soon burned
to a uniform deep ruddy brown, only a shade paler
than the native crew.

We were in the tropics now. The ocean was of a
vivid blue that I had never seen. Shoals of flying

fish rose before the Tara's cutwater to skim off above the waves, and sometimes the water about us was alive with the predatory fish which rove the open sea. One afternoon Marama showed me how to catch my first albicore in native fashion.

We were standing by the rail, on the after deck. Suddenly, close to the schooner's side, a dozen great steel-blue fish flashed into the air, leaping like porpoises. "Albicore!" exclaimed my companion, as he darted away toward the forecastle. A moment later he was back, brandishing a twelve-foot pole of heavy bamboo. To the small end of it he made fast a length of strong cotton line, terminating in a lure of mother-of-pearl tinted in iridescent shades of yellow and green and fitted with a barbless hook of brass. The shell was cut and polished to resemble a six-inch flying-fish, with a tuft of white horsehair projecting on either side to represent the wings.

The albicore were still leaping and flashing alongside, now darting ahead, now circling to follow in our wake. Marama tossed his lure overboard and allowed it to skitter on the waves, holding the butt of the rod strongly with both hands. There was a flash of blue in the sea; the lure disappeared; the line snapped taut; the bamboo bent with the struggles of a powerful fish. A yell burst from my companion's lips. He braced himself to heave with all his strength, and a thirty-pound albicore, vibrant and flashing in the sunlight, broke from the water, sailed over the rail, and thudded to the deck.

"Quick!" shouted Marama. "You try! I kill this one — take him forward — Seroni no like blood on deck."

My own blood was up and the hint was enough. In an instant the lure was overboard and I was doing my best with unskilled hands to make it skitter as the native boy had done. The fish had circled and were following astern; I could see the spray of their leaping in the schooner's wake. Then, as I gazed into the clear water, I saw a single monstrous albicore rushing at my hook. His jaws gaped wide — there was a mighty wrench; I found myself doubled over the rail, clinging to the rod with all my strength and shouting for help. Marama had turned to come aft and his quick eye took in the situation at a glance. He bounded to the forecastle and came running along the deck, holding aloft a long, four-pointed spear. *"Tapea maitai!"* he shouted — "Don't let go!" At that moment, Seroni himself — for that was my uncle's native name — appeared on deck. He seized the spear from Marama's hand and sprang to the rail. I was beginning to learn that Uncle Harry prided himself on excelling the natives in their own pursuits. His arm shot out in a swift dexterous thrust which transfixed the wallowing fish, so heavy that we could not lift it till a noose had been thrown over its tail.

That night, for the first time in my life, I tasted the characteristic dish of Polynesia: raw fillets of fish, soaked in vinegar and served as an appetizer.

The trade wind held for sixteen days, and when it died away at last we were only four hundred miles north of the Line. Then the Tara's sails were furled and for three days and three nights the engine drove us southward over a sea ruffled by light airs from the west. I shall never forget those equatorial nights, when all the others, saving the steersman and myself, were asleep on deck — the steady pulsing of the Tara's motor; the calm sea, heaving gently as a sleeper's breast; the Southern Cross, low down among the blazing constellations. Each day at dawn the air cooled and freshened; presently the sky to the east began to pale, the little clouds on the horizon grew luminous with rosy light, and the sun appeared above the rim of the sea, a disk of dazzling brightness, glaring like burnished brass. The sunsets, on evenings when masses of cloud were piled along the western sky, were still more beautiful. Long after the sun had sunk beyond the slope of the world the clouds were tinted with opal and rose, and pierced by lofty shafts of golden light.

We crossed the Line and met the southeast trade, blowing from the far-off Chilean coast. Then the sheets were close-hauled and the Tara began to beat southward, pitching and bucking into the head sea. Marama brought racks to hold the dishes on our table; we moved about the deck in short runs, grasping at the rail or a convenient stay; and for the first time I felt a landsman's seasick qualms. The constant tossing made all hands irritable, and brought on the trouble between Pahuri and the cook.

I heard from Marama how the affair began. Fatu and the engineer ate their meals forward with the men, old friends and natives like themselves, with whom there was no occasion to enforce strict discipline. Pahuri, the little Rarotongan engineer, was the oldest man and the recognized story-teller of the crew. He had seen many strange parts of the world, and no doubt, like other story-tellers I have known, he was quite ready to describe other places he had never seen. No matter how often the story had been told, nor how obviously embellished by a resourceful imagination, the men always listened eagerly when Pahuri began his tale. Rairi, the half-caste cook, was the only skeptic of the lot, and his comment on the engineer's accounts of Sydney and Wellington and Singapore, coupled with his own white blood and pretense of superiority, caused daily friction between the two. There was soup on the day of the trouble, scalding-hot soup, carried to the forecastle by Rairi's own hands, and a plate of it, poured down the engineer's neck when the Tara gave a sudden violent lurch, brought Pahuri raging to his feet. Rairi was Paumotan on the native side; to a man of his kind no epithet could have been more offensive than the engineer's angry: "*Uri Paumotu!* — Paumotan dog!" But the mate's presence tied his hands and he retired sullenly to the galley, trembling with rage. The sequel came late that night.

Pahuri had been working on his engine and he came on deck, a little after midnight, for a breath of air. He was leaning on the rail by the shrouds when strong hands seized his throat and he heard a fierce whisper in his ear:—

"Ah! — Pig of a Rarotongan!"

Pahuri was a wiry little man and he struggled frantically in the other's grasp, for he realized at once that the cook intended to strangle him into silence and heave him overboard. He twisted his body about, gripped the shrouds like a monkey, doubled up his knees and drove both heels into Rairi's stomach. The cook relaxed his hands for a moment with a grunt of pain, and Pahuri managed to give a stifled shout. But the half-caste's fingers tightened once more, and the engineer felt his senses leaving him. His hands fell from the shrouds to which he had clung, his body was lifted to the height of the rail, and he thought numbly that the end was near. Then, suddenly as he had been seized, he was dropped to the deck, where he lay gasping for a time before he realized what had occurred.

The giant mate was standing over him, gazing down with an expression of concern. There was a waning moon, and by its light Pahuri saw that Fatu held the cook with one huge outstretched hand, the thumb and fingers sunk in the half-caste's corded neck. He held him easily as one lifts a puppy by the scruff.

"What is this?" the mate asked mildly, in his

soft deep voice. "Has this man tried to do you
harm?"

The man at the wheel had given the alarm, and
my uncle came on deck a moment later, dressed
only in a pareu, his chest and powerful shoulders
bare. I had been sleeping, but the noises of the
scuffle awakened me, and I followed close behind.
Pahuri was able to speak when we arrived and he
told a story that left out no detail of the affair.
For a moment, no one thought of the half-caste,
struggling weakly in Fatu's mighty grip. Even in
the moonlight, I could see that his face was black-
ening — I pointed and touched my uncle's arm.

"Let him go, Fatu!" he ordered sharply. "You'll
kill the man!"

The mate had been listening intently to Pahuri's
tale, and at Uncle Harry's words he dropped Rairi
with an air of surprise, as if he had forgotten him.
The cook had fainted; we could not revive him
until a bucket of sea water had been dashed over
his face. At that he sat up feebly, groaning as his
hands went up to feel his neck. My uncle glanced
down, his dark eyes burning with a glitter that
made Rairi turn away his face.

"Feel better now?" asked my uncle in a hard
vibrant voice. "I'm glad of that, for I've something to say to you. You understand English, eh?
You need n't do any talking — I know all about
this affair. You tried to kill Pahuri — an old man
half your size and your superior on board. These
boys would like to heave you into the sea; I fancy

they're right, it would be a riddance of damned
poor trash. The only difficulty is that I need a
cook. We're going to Raiatea first, and if you value
your skin, you'll stick close aboard. Then I'm
going to Tahiti and I'll drop you there. If you
behave yourself from now on, I'll say nothing to
the authorities; but if you try any more tricks, if
any member of the crew goes overboard accident-
ally at night, or if anyone so much as falls ill before
we reach Tahiti, I'll feel it my duty to turn you
over to the French, who know me well. They guil-
lotine their murderers down there — it's not a
pleasant way to die! Think it over. You can go
forward now."

Rairi struggled to his feet and tottered forward
with a hand on the rail. At that moment, moved
by a boy's emotion, I felt almost sorry for him, but
as he passed me I caught a glimpse of his face in
the moonlight — dark handsome features distorted
by passion. I drew back as if he had raised his hand
to strike me, but the others had not seen what I
had seen, and I stifled the cry of warning which
rose to my lips.

There was no more trouble with Rairi while he
remained aboard the Tara; he went about his duties
in silence, ignored by the sailors and sitting alone
in his galley during the slack hours of the day.
But I know now that it would have been better for
us, and better for him, perhaps, in the long run, if
my uncle had given his men their way — had let
them throw the revengeful half-caste to the sharks.

On the morning after the trouble we raised our first land — the western islands of the Marquesas. At sunset we had seen flocks of birds flying steadily southeast, and my uncle told me that if we followed them they would lead us to the land. At dawn, when I came on deck, I heard the ringing shout of landfall from aloft, and gazing eastward, I made out the high silhouette of Hatutu, a faint outline against the flushing sky. An hour later we drew abreast of Eiao, a saw-toothed ridge, falling away gently at either end; and toward midday we raised the rock of Motu Iti, and the long highlands of Nukuhiva, veiled in masses of black thundercloud. At nightfall, in the darkling east, the pinnacled skyline of Uapou faded and disappeared.

"A beautiful group," remarked my uncle, standing by the rail. "When I was trading there I knew every bay from Hanavave to Tai-O-Hae. The larger islands have a fascination — a gloomy beauty that gets into one's blood. The people, though they were cannibals, were a fine savage race, who had developed, during the course of centuries in their isolated group, an interesting culture of their own. But their blood was too wild to stand contact with our civilization, and when the white man came they died off, as the Indian and the buffalo disappeared from our American plains. Now the valleys where people once dwelt in thousands are silent and deserted, the lonely burial-places of a vanished race. I suppose I'm a heathen, but I can see the savage's point of view — he asked no more than to be left in peace, a favor we white men have never been willing to grant . . . ."

Two days afterward I had my first glimpse of the coral islands. The moon was bright that evening as we passed through the twelve-mile channel separating the atolls of Rangiroa and Tikehau. I climbed to a perch in the shrouds and lingered there as we coasted the western end of Rangiroa; the night-breeze blowing off the land brought to my nostrils a faint sweet perfume, the odor of pandanus blossoms. The line of palms, growing on the low ring of land, stood out sharply in the moonlight, and at times, when we passed a region of sparser vegetation, I had glimpses of the great lagoon beyond, silvered by the moon and stretching away to the horizon without land in sight.

It was close to midnight when the atoll dropped away astern and I climbed down to the deck, stiff from my long vigil aloft. I found Uncle Harry busy over some papers at the little desk in his stateroom. He swung about in his chair and lit a cigar as I sat down on the berth.

"Been having a look at Rangiroa, eh," he remarked. "There's a kind of beauty about the atolls, especially on a moonlight night. Iriatai is the same sort of place, though on a much smaller scale. There's no other group in the world like the Paumotus: eighty lagoon islands, some of them of immense size, strung out northwest and southeast in a cluster a thousand miles long. Darwin believed that they were the peaks of a submerged

mountain-range, on which the coral polyps have
built, as the mountains sank little by little beneath
the sea. The lagoons are accounted for on the
ground that the polyps tend to die in calm water,
and thrive best in the froth and spray of breaking
seas. As time went on, you see, the ones on the
outside would build higher and higher, while the
ones inside would die. Then, as the island con-
tinued gradually to sink, with the live polyps all
working in the wash of the sea along the outer rim,
a deepening lagoon would form inside — and there
you have your atoll. The passes are believed to
be caused by fresh water, the heavy rainfall of
these latitudes, finding an outlet to the sea. Running out at low tide over the lowest portion of the
reef, it kills the coral-builders and causes the slow
formation of a pass, often deep enough to allow
large vessels to enter the lagoon.

"There was a day, perhaps, two thousand years
ago, when the Paumotus lay lonely and uninhabited, spread out like a vast net, a thousand
miles long and four hundred miles across, to catch
the canoes of wanderers who had missed the higher
and richer islands to the west. The Polynesians
were daring seamen, but their methods of naviga-
tion were of the most primitive sort — by the stars,
the clouds, the trade wind, and the flight of birds.
Hundreds of their great double canoes with clumsy
sails of matting must have left Samoa for the eastern groups, and some of them, missing the Cook
Islands or Tahiti, of which they had only half-

legendary accounts, fetched up along this chain of atolls. The Paumotan people of to-day are their descendants. The names of the islands still show the wonder of those ancient wanderers at the strange sea in which they found themselves, and the joy and relief the landfalls brought — 'The Spread-out Heavens'; 'The Place of Rejoicing'; 'The Windward Rainbow'; 'The Land of Great Beacon-Fires.' But perhaps this does n't interest you very much — I have a way of preaching when I start on the subject of the islands!" My uncle tilted his chair and smiled at me through a cloud of smoke.

"The wind is shifting toward the north," he went on, "and with a little luck we 'll sight Raiatea before dark to-morrow night. As I said, I 'll leave young Marama with you; you 're getting on well with the language, but you 'll need an interpreter for the present. I 'll be gone a month, at least, and when I return I 'd like to be able to start at once for Iriatai. You 'll stop with Marama's father, the chief of Faatemu Bay. I 'll be careful to explain what I want to the old man, but remember that a native has n't the least notion of the passage of time. I 'm leaving this to you — if you don't keep after old Taura every day, the canoes may not be finished for months. I want fifteen strongly made canoes of hibiscus wood, about twenty feet long, and complete with outriggers, cinnet for lashings, and a pair of paddles with each. Then we 'll need twenty-five or thirty pairs of diving-goggles, with the glass set in wood or horn. Some of the men will have their own, but they're always losing them, and once his goggles are lost, a diver is no more use. I'll leave you the glass and the diamond to cut it with; Marama will find you men who understand this work. I have a store at Faatemu; you can take the keys and advance a certain amount of goods to the canoe-builders, but don't let them get too far ahead of you! Old Taura, the chief, is as good a native as I know, and he'll see that you enjoy your stay on the island. You'll be swimming, and spearing fish, and hunting wild pig in the mountains — I only wish that I were stopping over, myself!"

The north wind blew all night with sudden fierce gusts and squalls of rain. The day broke wild and gray, but toward noon the sun shone out, and presently the clouds were left behind, sinking along the horizon to the north. At four bells land was in sight — the peaks of Huahine, bearing a little west of south, minute irregularities on the line where sea met sky. It was an afternoon such as one sees rarely in the tropics: a cloudless horizon and an atmosphere clear as the air above our deserts at home. An hour before sundown the Leeward Islands were all in view, strung out in the shape of a great half-moon on the sea ahead of us. The tall mountain rising abruptly in the north was Bora Bora; Tahaa and Raiatea, sheltered within the same circling barrier-reef, lay straight before the Tara's bows; and Huahine made the southern horn — beautiful as some land remembered from a dream.

At midnight we saw the torches of fishermen on the Raiatea reef, and dawn found us off Faatemu Bay. The sails were furled, Pahuri started the engine, and we glided in through the Nao Nao passage, past the green islet of Haaio, past Tuuroto Point, and into the deep inlet where the thatched roofs of the village clustered beneath the palms.

IV

AT FAATEMU

I wish that I had space to tell more of the month I spent at Faatemu — the story of all that happened in those days would fill a thicker volume than this one. I was young, keenly alive, and set down among strange and kindly people in a brand-new world. When the Tara set sail at nightfall I felt a little lonely and forlorn, but before another day had passed I was beginning to enjoy one of the happiest periods of my life. No matter how far I wander, or how remote those dreamy island days, I shall never forget the kindness of my friends, the brown Faatemu villagers.

We had been sighted offshore and canoes were thick about the Tara when her anchor dropped. Taura was the first man aboard — a stately, gray-haired native, of a type not common nowadays. He was barefoot, but his suit of drill was spotless and he wore a beautifully plaited hat. His fat old wife Hina came behind him, her kindly face working and her eyes full of tears; and Tetua, Marama's little sister, stood shyly at her mother's side. Hina made straight for her son and clung to him for a time, sobbing gently; Tetua kissed her brother bashfully; and finally the chief, after he had shaken hands with the rest of us, sat down beside Marama for the silent greeting of their race.

"Come ashore with me," called my uncle, as the ship's boat went over the side; "there's some copra here and I still have room for a bit of deck cargo. We must hurry if I'm going to get away to-night!"

The boat plied back and forth all morning, laden with bags of copra, while Uncle Harry unlocked his store, showed me how to keep account of the goods, and explained to Taura that I was to stop over and that the canoe-building must be hurried as much as possible. The chief promised to have the canoes ready in a month's time. As for divers, he believed we could pick up all we needed on Raiatea — Paumotu men who had settled in the Leeward group. My bag and light blanket were brought ashore and installed in Taura's house, and toward evening my uncle bade us good-bye and was pulled out to the schooner. It was dusk when she stole out through the pass, before the gentle night-breeze which comes down from the hills.

I lay awake long that night, in my bed in a corner of Taura's great single room. The others had spread a mat on the floor and set a turned-down lamp near by. Father, mother, and sister lay in a circle about Marama while he recounted, in a low voice and with many gestures, the story of his adventures in the north. I lay staring up at the rafters under the lofty thatch, thinking of all that had happened since Uncle Harry had steered his boat in through the California surf; of the von Tesmars, father and son; of Iriatai, and what the

future held in store. The lamp flickered when the
land breeze found its way through the thin bamboo walls, causing the shadows above me to deepen
and retreat; Marama's rapid flow of words droned
on monotonously; and at last sleep closed my eyes.

Early next day, when Taura came to demand
half a dozen axes for his men, I did my first bit of
trading. Then I closed the store, and Marama
and I went with the canoe-builders to select
their trees in the valley far up among the
mountains. We followed the river up from the
bay toward Faaroa, the great central valley of the
island. A dim path, along which we walked in
single file, led through the jungle, winding about
the trunks of fallen trees, across the rushing, waist-
deep stream, high along the mountain-side, at a
place where the valley became a gorge. I saw
thickets of *fei*, the wild plantain, bearing great
bunches of its reddish fruit; jungle cock crowed
shrilly among the hills; and once a troop of wild
pig, led by a gray old boar, crashed off, grunting,
through the undergrowth. It was strange to think
that only three generations had passed since Marama's ancestors, fierce brown warriors armed with
rude ironwood clubs and spears, had stolen along
this same path on forays against neighboring clans.

The wild hibiscus seldom grows large enough
to furnish a log for a twenty-foot canoe, and it
took us the best part of the day to choose our trees.
All were close enough to be dragged to the river
and floated down to Faatemu, and while the work

was going on Marama and I went out every day
with the men. First of all, the tree was felled and
the branches chopped off smoothly, flush with the
trunk. Then a twenty-foot length was measured
along the straightest part of the tree and the ends
cut off, before the log was rolled and dragged to
the riverside. Finally, when our fifteen logs were
ready, it took a strenuous day's work, pushing
over shallow reaches and swimming through deep
pools, to float them to the beach.

Once our logs were at Faatemu, Taura was for
giving a feast and resting for a day or two. But
I urged haste, recalling my uncle's words to the
chief. Then the logs were laid out in the shade,
close to the village, and one man set to work on
each, fashioning a canoe with axe and adze. Day
after day the builder chopped, while the chips flew
and the form of the canoe emerged — the curve
of sheer, the rounded bilge, the sharp lines of bow
and stern. Sometimes a man stood off, squinting
at his handiwork with one eye closed — judging
the symmetry of the slender hull. When the outside was roughly chopped to shape, the log was
turned over and the builder began to hollow out
the inside with his adze. At last, when the walls
of wood were of the required thickness, the process
of finishing began: a slow and laborious rubbing
with hard bits of coral, and a final smoothing with
the rough skin of a stingray's tail, tacked to a
wooden block. Then a pair of narrow planks of
hibiscus were sawn out to make the raised gun-

wales, six inches high and of the same thickness as the sides of the canoe. After long scraping and repeated trials, these gunwales were made to fit so perfectly that no crack of light appeared when they were set in place. At intervals of about a foot, holes were drilled in the gunwales and corresponding holes in the dugout-sides beneath. The planks were joined at stem and stern and lashed to the canoe with cinnet — strong cording made of the braided fibre of the coconut. Now, save for its outrigger, the canoe was finished.

Round-bottomed and very narrow for their length, the native canoes would capsize at once were it not for their outriggers — light slender logs which float in the water alongside at a distance of four or five feet, attached to the hull by a pair of transverse poles. When Captain Cook first sailed among the islands, the natives marveled at the great canoe which remained upright without an outrigger — more wonderful by far, in their eyes, than the white man's cannon, or muskets, or axes of steel. "*Aué!*" they exclaimed, in astonishment. "*E vaa ama oré!*" — a canoe without an outrigger!

We made our outriggers of light *purau* wood, twenty feet long, five or six inches thick, and pointed at the forward end. The attaching poles were of ironwood — *casuarina* is the name of the beautiful, pale-foliaged tree — lashed across the gunwales fore and aft, the bow pole rigid, the rear one curved and flexible. At Taura's suggestion, I gave orders that all the outriggers and their fittings be assembled, and the canoes tested in the water before they were taken apart to be loaded aboard the Tara. Thanks to the chief, they were ready some days before the schooner came in sight, and our diving-goggles, made in the evenings by the old men of the village, were finished and waiting at the store.

To the native fisherman, these goggles are nearly as important as his spear. They are not unlike the goggles used by motorists at home: a pair of glasses, set in wooden rims which fit tightly about one's eyes, and held in place by an elastic around the head. With such glasses, well fitted and water-tight, one can see nearly as well in the clear sea-water as in the air above.

I kept two pairs for Marama and myself, and we went out often, on afternoons of leisure, to spear fish inside the reef. Paddling to a place where the water was from five to ten feet deep, we moored our canoe to a coral mushroom and set out, swimming for long distances or wading as the water shoaled. Little by little I learned one of the most difficult of native arts: to swim gently with my face under water, holding the spear between my toes. I learned to distinguish the good fish from the bad, the wholesome from the poisonous; to recognize the holes where the fat black *maito* hide; to see the octopus dart into his cranny; to transfix my quarry with a well-aimed thrust. Sometimes we were in the water for three hours at a stretch, but I never wearied of admiring the strange beauty of this underwater world. The sunlight, filtering through the clear lagoon and reflected from the bottom in delicate tints of blue and green, revealed shoals of fish, colored like jewels and of fantastic shapes, gliding among the branches of the coral forest. In deeper water a gleam of vivid blue showed where the tridacna — the giant clam — lay in his hole with jaws agape, and I learned to swim down with a bar of steel and pry him from the rock.

Sometimes, on moonless nights, we took torches and went out spearing on the reef. The Raiatea barrier-reef, about a mile offshore, is no more than a low dyke of coral, half awash and breaking the landward run of the swell. By night, when the torches flicker and flare, and mighty combers, bursting on the outer edge, come foaming waist-deep across the jagged rock, the reef is an eerie place, not without dangers of its own. Under cover of darkness, strange monsters have been known to crawl up from the depths on the seaward side — the huge decapods on which the sperm whale feeds, and nameless creatures of which the natives speak with whispered dread. There were tales of fishermen who had paddled out at nightfall, never to return. . . . Nothing would have tempted me to fish on the reef alone at night, though when several of us went out together, armed with machetes and heavy spears, there was a wild charm about the sport.

We walked abreast in a line that reached from

lagoon to sea, each man bearing in his left hand a torch of dry bamboo. At times, a cry from the seaward man caused us to brace ourselves for the big sea he had seen rearing in the torchlight. Then with a roar and a crash the wave would break, sending a wall of white water across the barrier. Sometimes a shark came thrashing across with the wave, to be speared before he could reach the deep water of the lagoon. Sometimes a series of shouts went up as a great silver cavally swept by us so fast that man after man missed his thrust. When the wave receded there were spiny crayfish to be caught in the pools, and enormous pink-spotted crabs to be held down with a spear-shaft till one could take a safe grip, out of reach of the menacing claws.

One day, when the sun was bright and the current in the pass was slack, Marama showed me a pleasanter and lazier kind of fishing. He had caught a great quantity of hermit crabs the night before, and at daybreak I found him on the beach, picking up the pebbles used for sinkers and tossing them into the bottom of the canoe. He had brought a line fitted with strong hooks on wire leaders, and his water glass — a small wooden box, open at the top and with a bottom made of a pane of clear glass. We paddled to the passage and anchored the canoe on one side, where she could swing out over the wall of coral, shelving almost vertically into deep blue water. Then Marama began to crack the shells of his crabs, smash the claws and bodies between two stones, and toss this ground bait over the side of the canoe. I took the glass and watched the fragments of crab-meat eddying down beside the seamed and crannied wall. The water was so clear that every detail of the scene was visible: the strange fish drifting along the face of the cliff; the mouths of the caverns from which larger fish looked out; the sandy bottom beneath us, scoured clean by the current of the pass. At first, only a shoal of small fry gathered to gobble up the bait, but suddenly they scattered in terror as a pair of parrot fish, bright blue and a yard long, with horny beaks instead of mouths, moved leisurely from their hiding-place. There was so little wind that my companion had seen them without his glass. He baited his hook with the soft body of a hermit crab, tied a pebble to his line with the curious hitch that allows the sinker to be released by a jerk, and dropped hook and stone over the side. I watched the pebble rush down toward the bottom; saw it halt below the drifting bait; saw the line jerk and the sinker drop off and disappear; watched the baited hook rise slowly to the level of the parrot fish, that were beginning to feed in their deliberate way.

Now Marama's bait was eddying among the other morsels of crab, and I almost shouted as I saw it disappear in the beak of the larger of the big blue fish. The native boy struck sharply and began to haul in his line, cutting the water in crisp zigzags this way and that. A final heave brought the twenty-pound fish tumbling into the canoe, a blow of a short club ended its struggles, and I examined it at leisure while Marama baited his hook once more. It was the first that I had seen — a strange and beautiful creature, covered with scales larger than a fifty-cent piece, scales of a vivid iridescent blue with a green spot at the base of each. A nip of its horny beak would have severed a man's finger clean. Later that day when I ate my share of it, steaming-hot from the oven, I understood why the parrot fish was prized so highly.

When Taura's family assembled for a meal, all of their cooked food came from the native oven, under the shed behind the house. Their method of cooking seemed to me — and still seems, when I think of those dinners at Faatemu — the finest in the world, preserving as it does all the juices and flavor of fish or fowl or meat. The native cook's equipment consists of a heap of waterworn pebbles, picked up along the beach, a pile of large green leaves, and a supply of firewood. Fish and chicken and pork are cut into pieces of convenient size and made into little leaf-wrapped packages. Yams, sweet potatoes, plantains, and bananas are selected for cooking and laid out beside the packages of meat. Then a shallow hole is scraped out in the earth — perhaps a foot deep, and two feet across — and a hot fire is built inside. When the fire is blazing well, the pebbles are heaped on the wood and left till they are heated almost to a glow. At this stage the hole is raked out clean, the food put in and covered with hot pebbles, and the whole overlaid with a thick layer of leaves and earth. An hour later the oven may be opened, the baked vegetables peeled, and the packages of fish and meat removed from their clean leafy wrappings.

As time went on, it seemed to me that my friend Marama possessed more useful accomplishments than any lad of his age at home. The fishing excursions in which I was always eager to join were in reality his work, for we supplied more than half of the household's food. My friend could read and write, but otherwise he had no education in our sense of the word. He knew nothing of history, algebra, or geometry, but his mind was a storehouse of complex fishing-lore, picked up unconsciously since babyhood and enabling him to provide himself and his family with food. And when you come to think of it, that is one of the purposes of all education.

The habits of the fish in the South Pacific are regulated by the moon, and Marama knew what kinds were to be found on any night of the native lunar month. On nights of bright moonlight we cast a white fly for the small rockfish which frequent patches of live coral; on dark nights we gathered the mollusks abounding in the lagoon. During the week of the new moon's first appearance, we went out at dawn to fish for tunny in the pass. Sometimes Tetua, the twelve-year-old sister of Marama, took me with her to spear prawns in the Faatemu River. Carrying torches and armed with small barbless spears, we slipped and clambered over the wet rocks, scanning the pools for the little fresh-water lobsters which soon filled our pail. Sometimes I took a paddle in one of the long narrow bonito-canoes and went with the men on trips that took us far offshore, following the birds above the leaping schools. I grew hard and browned by the sun, and the native language came to me surprisingly.

Once on a Saturday, when my uncle's work was done, Taura took us to the mountains to hunt for pig. The chief's two lean dogs ranged ahead, and far up in the Faaroa Valley they started a bristling gray boar, fierce, old, and fleet of foot. He led us a long chase over the rough stream-bed and through dense thickets of tree-fern and hibiscus. In the end we heard a fierce uproar of snarls and yelps and grunting, and knew that he had turned at bay. Taura was too old to run as we did, and by this time the chief was a good half-mile behind. We had no weapons, and when I saw the angry brute, foam dripping from his jaws as he faced the dogs with his back to a great tree-trunk, I wondered what we were to do, now that we had come up with him. But Marama did not share my hesitation.

"Take care!" he warned me — unnecessarily, I thought. "He is a bad pig! If he runs at you, jump into a tree!"

He took a clasp knife from the tuck of his pareu, cut a limb of hibiscus, and peeled off a length of the tough bark — the strongest of natural cord. Then he shouted encouragingly to the dogs, and while their attack diverted the boar's attention, he stole quickly around the sheltering tree-trunk. I saw his brown hands shoot out to seize the boar's hind legs, and the next moment — grunting and struggling ferociously — the old brute was thrown heavily upon his back. I rushed to lend a hand and our combined strength was enough to hold him while we tied his legs with strips of bark. Taura found us lying exhausted beside our captive, while the dogs lay in the cool stream, with heaving flanks and tongues lolling in the water.

That evening, when Marama had recounted the details of our hunt, his mother told us one of her tales of heathen days — the story of how the first pigs were given by the ancient gods to mankind. Many of her words I understood; at times her son whispered a translation in rapid broken English. We were lying on a wide mat, spread under the palms close to the beach. A new moon was setting behind the point and the evening was so calm that only the faintest of murmurs came from the reef.

There was a time — so the story ran — many years ago, when there were no pigs on any of these islands. In those days men ate only fish, and sometimes, in seasons of famine, the flesh of rats. The clans of the different valleys were constantly at war, for there was no one government over the island — no family of Raiatean chiefs. Men lost heart for the planting when villages were destroyed and crops burned on every hand, and many of the people left their lands to live in hidden caves among the hills.

In this bay of Faatemu lived a feeble old man, blind with age and weeping, for his wife and all but one of his children had been slaughtered in the wars. He was called Vatea, and the name of his young son, who cared for him, was Tamatoa. They lived in a rude thatch-shelter the boy had built. It was a time of famine; a war-party from Tahaa had burned the village, and there were no plantations of yams or sweet potatoes. The men of Tahaa, as was their custom, had chopped down all the coconut palms, and Tamatoa feared to go after plantains. By day the father and son kept to their hidden shelter, and each night the boy came cautiously to the seaside, to catch what fish he could. Since he dared not use a torch, that was not much; on many occasions his patience was rewarded by no more than one small fish. Then he would make for himself a poor dish of scraped banana-stalks, not fit to keep the life in a man, and after preparing his single fish, he would carry the food to where blind old Vatea awaited him. "I have caught only two small fish," he told the old man at these times; "one for you, and one for me. Now let us eat!" And while the hungry father devoured his fish, the son would make a great noise of smacking his own lips over the wretched scrapings of banana stalk.

Each day the fish were smaller and more difficult

to catch, and finally the old man was starving, though Tamatoa gave him all the real food that he could find. As happens at such times, Vatea grew suspicious of his son, thinking that the boy was taking advantage of his blindness to save the best morsels for himself. One day, when the son brought a small raw fish and his own dish of grated banana-stalk, the old man spoke. 'Fetch me a calabash of cool water from the stream,' he said; and when the boy was gone, he felt his way across to where his son's food lay in a wooden bowl. Then his tears fell, and his heart was heavy with remorse.

That night, as they lay side by side on their mats, old Vatea spoke to his son. "Listen carefully to my words," he said, "and forget nothing that I say. To-morrow I shall die; when I am dead, bury me by the great rosewood tree yonder in the valley. Then, every morning, you shall go to my grave at the hour when the sun first strikes the ground. Watch closely; take what you find and use it wisely — it will make you a powerful man."

Next morning old Vatea died, and his son, who was a dutiful lad, did as the father had instructed. For two days, when the first rays of sunlight touched his father's grave he was watching by the rosewood tree, and on the third morning his eyes saw a strange thing. The earth cracked and heaved, and he heard a new sound, the sound of grunting, as a pair of pigs came up out of the dust — the first pigs that any man had seen. Marveling greatly, Tamatoa took them home and cared for them, and only a day or two later, peace was made among the clans, and a bountiful run of fish entered the lagoon.

Litters of young pigs were born as time went on, and the fame of Tamatoa went abroad among the islands — to Huahine, to Bora Bora, and even to distant Maupiti. Then the high priest of Oro, at the Opoa temple, was seized with a frenzy, and through his lips the chiefs learned that Tamatoa, the favored of the gods, was to be made ruler of the island. Thus Tamatoa became king, and the race of swine was given to furnish food for men.

As she finished the story, Marama's mother heaved herself to her feet and led the way to Taura's steep-roofed house. The moon had set, and as I followed through the warm darkness, I thought drowsily of my uncle and wondered when the Tara would return. I might have slept less soundly if I had known that she was then within twenty miles, and that in the morning she would anchor in Faatemu Bay.

V
IRIATAI

I was awakened at daybreak by a noise of shouting, and running out of the house, my eyes still heavy with sleep, I saw the Tara standing in through the Nao Nao Pass. I called to Marama. We launched our canoe and paddled out as the schooner rounded to and dropped anchor with a prolonged rattle of chain. My uncle was standing at the wheel — a tall bronzed figure in a scarlet waist-cloth; he called out a jovial greeting as we paddled alongside. Ivi and Ofai were busy with the whaleboat; Fatu waved an enormous hand at us; I saw Pahuri standing by the rail, smiling his cynical and wrinkled smile.

"Come aboard, boys," my uncle shouted. "Eh, Charlie, the islands agree with you, I see! You're brown as a native and an inch broader than when I saw you last! Hello, Marama! *Mai ai oe?* How's the work coming on? All the canoes ready?"

It seemed like returning home, to breakfast once more in the Tara's saloon. Uncle Harry was in high spirits at the prospect of an early start. Everything had been arranged in Tahiti; the Tara's cargo had been unloaded, and a fresh cargo — all our supplies for the diving-season on Iriatai — taken aboard.

"An odd thing happened," remarked my uncle

as we sat down. "I lost a lot of papers from my desk. Remember the letter I translated to you at home — the one about Iriatai, from the old native woman to her son? Well, that was among them; it's of no use to anyone, of course, now that we have the lagoon tied up. A piece of spite-work, I think. Rairi, that precious cook of ours, boarded the schooner one day while I was ashore — said he'd forgotten a bundle of his things.

"I wish you'd been with me," he went on, "you'd have had a look at a famous schooner and the most picturesque scoundrel in the South Seas. Ever hear of Thursday Island Schmidt? Oh yes, I remember — I mentioned him that night at the ranch. Well, this was my first glimpse of him, and I'll own that I was interested. A week ago he brought his little schooner into Papeete with a load of shell from the Gambier Islands. She's as pretty as her reputation is black, and the way he handled her was a treat to watch. She's flying the tricolor now; he transferred her to French registry in Nou-mea, last year. They know less than the British about her past! She's dodged Russian gunboats when Schmidt was seal-poaching in the foggy North Pacific; she's kidnapped wild bush-niggers, out in the Solomons and New Hebrides; she's posed as an Australian revenue-boat to hold up the Malay pearlers in Torres Straits, where her skipper got his name. I saw Schmidt in the club that afternoon — he's a big German, with a full beard and a pair of cold blue eyes. They say he's a cashiered naval officer — a great talker at any rate, and speaks English like a professor.

"Papeete's a gossipy place! After Schmidt had left the club, I heard some queer yarns. There's a rumor that he has a prisoner aboard the Cholita — someone who's never allowed ashore and whom visitors are never allowed to see! The traders have nothing to think about but the price of copra, and other men's affairs!

"One night on the water-front I saw Schmidt walking with a man I thought was Rairi, but the native turned away before I was close enough to make sure, and old Thursday Island gave me a long stare as I passed under a street lamp. By Jove! It set me to thinking, you know! Suppose Rairi has the letter — he may be cooking up some deviltry with the master of the Cholita! I'll be nervous as an old woman till I get that shell safely stowed away! But that's nonsense — we're living in the twentieth century, and even if Rairi knows more than is good for him, Thursday Island would n't dare try any of his old tricks nowadays.

"Come," concluded Uncle Harry, who had been talking as I breakfasted, "we must be getting ashore. Fatu can bring the canoes out and stow them away while we have a yarn with the chief. I hope he has found me some divers."

Taura had sent word to the small Paumotan settlements scattered around the island, and for a week past the divers had been drifting in to Faatemu, traveling by cutter or sailing-canoe with their women, their children, and their household goods. My uncle went to their camp to select his men, and soon the bay was a lively place, echoing with laughter and shouts as the laden canoes plied between the schooner and the beach. The Tara, once smart as a yacht, took on the aspect of a floating menagerie: pigs grunted disconsolately on deck; dogs barked; hens clucked; roosters crowed. A swarm of Paumotans lay about, smoking, chattering in high-pitched voices, playing accordions. The decks were littered with their mats and bedding, on which small brown babies lay asleep, unconscious of the uproar of departure.

Late in the afternoon Marama and I made our parting gifts to his family and paddled out to where the Tara lay, her engine going and her anchor up. We clambered over the rail; old Taura stood in the canoe, waving his hat while the schooner got under way and glided out toward the pass. Months were to pass before we saw the gray-haired chief again.

My uncle laid his course due east, to pass between the great atoll of Fakarava and Faaite, the smaller island to the south. The fair weather held while the Tara threaded her way through the strange Sea of Atolls — the dangerous archipelago, dreaded by mariners since the Pacific was first explored. We passed the southern end of Fakarava, a lagoon like an inland sea, surrounded by a narrow ring of palms, passed Katiu and Tuanake, turned south to skirt the treacherous reefs of Makemo, were swept eastward by the current racing between

Nihiru and Marutea, and breathed freely once more as we turned north, past Reka Reka, the Island of Good Hope. Sometimes a low smudge of palms lay along the horizon; sometimes, with no land in sight, the Tara battled with the fierce uncharted currents of this maze of reefs; and there were days when a green glimmer in the sky told of the presence of some huge lagoon, hidden from our eyes by the curving slope of the world. In the open sea to the east of Reka Reka, the bad weather began.

The wind veered to the northwest — the storm wind the natives call the *toerau*. Black clouds closed above the Tara like a canopy; for two days and two nights she made heavy weather through squalls of wind and rain. My uncle spent much of his time at the rail, binoculars raised to scan the empty horizon east of us.

"We must be close to Iriatai," he said to me on the morning of the last day, "but in these shifting currents, and without a chance for a shot at the sun, it's hard to say just where we are! Risky business, this knocking about at night — if we don't raise the land to-day, I'm going to heave to."

I had been gazing idly at the clouds drifting overhead, and had noticed several flocks of sea birds, passing high above us, all heading southward. As my uncle spoke, another flock appeared in the north. He saw them, too, and shouted a command to alter the schooner's course.

"That's the third lot of birds I've seen this

morning," he remarked; "there's a chance that they are coming from Iriatai. We'll beat up to the north a bit, and have a look."

An hour later I heard a long-drawn cry from the crosstrees, and soon from the deck I made out the familiar atoll-landfall — a level dark line of palm-tops, low on the northern horizon. It was Iriatai.

The island differs from most of the atolls in that the pass is on the weather side. The lagoon is nearly circular, ten miles long and about eight across, and the surrounding land is composed of three long curving islands, separated by short stretches of reef over which the sea washes no more than knee-deep on a calm day. A dense growth of young palms — planted by my uncle — covered the islands, and just inside the pass, where von Tesmar's settlement had stood before the hurricane, I saw the loftier tops of the trees planted by Turia, the dead Paumotan woman. From a perch high up in the shrouds, gazing with the glasses toward the far end of the lagoon, I could make out the tall old palms of the islet where the woman and her child had fetched up in that long-ago storm. We were at the end of our voyage: somewhere between the islet and the reef lay the patch of gold-lipped shell planted by the strange Austrian wanderer!

That night we anchored the Tara off the village of my uncle's laborers, natives established on the island to plant and to make copra as the trees began to bear. Next morning, with a dozen fresh helpers gossiping on deck and a man at the mast-head to give us warning of shoals, the Tara sailed the length of the lagoon and found a berth close to the high islet at the farther end. Our divers made their camp on that ten-acre dot of land, shaded by old palms which had survived the hurricane.

While the divers floated their canoes ashore and set to work to lash on the outriggers, the other men launched the boats to transfer the schooner's cargo to the beach. The women and children went ashore at once, stacked their belongings in individual heaps, and busied themselves with plaiting the palm-fronds with which their houses would be thatched.

The younger women and some of the boys swarmed up the trees like monkeys, machete in hand, and soon the green fronds were crashing to the ground on every side. Their older companions chopped off the heavy butts and split each rib down the middle, making a pair of tough strips of fibrous wood, fringed along one side with the narrow leaves of the coconut. Squatting on their heels, while their fingers worked with marvelous rapidity and skill, the women braided these leaves together to form strips of coarse green matting, a foot wide and eight feet long. As each piece was finished it was stacked on the growing family pile. By night-fall the last of the canoes was assembled and they were hauled up in a line on the beach. The men were now ready for their task of housebuilding. In two days our village on the islet was complete.

They began by clearing the chosen site, a couple of acres in extent. There was a dense growth of wild hibiscus under the coconut palms, and as they chopped this away with axe and bush-knife, they took care to save the long straight poles which would be of use. Then each man selected the place for his house and set to work by himself. With the help of his wife and children he dug four holes and set the corner-posts, forked at the top to receive the long poles corresponding to plates. Midway between the corner-posts at each end of the house, a much taller post was set, to support the ridgepole. Then plates and ridgepole were laid on their forked supports and lashed in place with strips of tough hibiscus-bark. Next, the rafters were made fast at a steep pitch, laid at intervals of about a foot, and a similar light framework was lashed to the gable ends. At this stage the house was ready to be thatched.

Now the entire family went to the far end of the islet to cut armfuls of bark for tying on their thatch, and when a supply of this natural cord was on hand, they set up light temporary scaffoldings of poles and took their places, — the woman outside, the man inside the roof, — to lay the thatch of plaited fronds. Working from the eaves toward the ridgepole, the strips were laid on like shingles, each one overlapping by four or five inches the one beneath, with the split midrib tied firmly to each rafter that it crossed. After the roof, the gable ends were thatched; a doorway was framed on the leeward side, and a rustic siding of hibiscus wands, placed vertically as close together as they would go, was set up from ground to plates. Then the family gathered the snowy coral gravel on the beach and spread it several inches deep to make a floor. The house was finished — cool, airy, and weatherproof, beautifully adapted to an environment where lumber and corrugated iron were out of place.

But lumber and iron were necessary for our water supply, and while the natives were busy with their housebuilding, we set to work to build a long low shed, with a gutter along the lower edge of the roof, from which tin piping would conduct the rain water to a series of large connected tanks. The drinking-nuts would never suffice for such a gathering, and fresh water was the one important thing the islet lacked. We relied on the rains to furnish our supply, and the shed was to serve as a store, and as a warehouse for our shell, when that had been cleaned and sacked.

The building was finished on a Saturday, and that night the men went out in their canoes to fish. They were all Christians and they kept the Sabbath more religiously than most of us at home. The missionaries who had converted them were of the strict old Calvinist school, which taught that it was sinful to fish, or plant, or to do any kind of work on the day of rest. My uncle respected the divers' beliefs, but he had communicated his own restless energy to the members of the Tara's crew,

and on that Sunday, while the Paumotans dozed in
the shade of their new houses, we took the whaleboat on an excursion to explore the diving-grounds.
When we returned at sunset the others shook their
heads — in their eyes we had reaped the reward
of sacrilege, for our boating-party had come near
to ending tragically.

The lagoon was calm that morning, calm as an
inland lake, its surface ruffled at intervals by faint
catspaws from the north. Looking back toward
the pass, there was no land in sight — the blue
water met the sky in an unbroken line. Ahead of
us, at the northern end of the atoll, the seabeach
was little more than a mile away, and the thunder
of the breakers was borne to our ears, now loud,
now soft, on flaws of air. My uncle stood in the
stern and I sat beside him; Fatu was in the bow,
Ivi and Ofai at the oars. Once or twice Fatu motioned my uncle to change his course, to avoid the
coral mushrooms rising to within a few inches of
the surface, but in general the depth of the lagoon
varied from six to twenty fathoms. Gazing down
through the blue translucent water, I could see the
strange forms of growing coral far beneath us; and
sometimes, as the bottom turned sandy and the
water shoaled, the lagoon shaded to purest emerald
green. Clad only in a scarlet pareu, with his
bronzed back and shoulders bare, Uncle Harry was
leaning over the side, gazing intently at the bottom
through a water glass. He had given the word to
go slowly, and the men were resting on their oars.

"This is the place," he said; "we'll anchor here and let Ofai go down for a look."

While Fatu was paying out the anchor line, I took the glass and leaned over to see what I could make out. The water was about twelve fathoms deep, and far down beneath the whaleboat's keel I could distinguish the purple coral on the floor of the lagoon. Ofai, the Rangiroa boy, was preparing himself to dive. He coiled a long cotton line in the bottom of the boat, and made fast to one end of it a thirty-pound bulb of lead, like an enormous sinker. Then he adjusted his goggles and went over the side. While he lay in the water, drawing a series of deep breaths, Fatu passed him the weight. He allowed it to sink a yard beneath him, seized the rope between the toes of one foot, and took a grip, high up on the line, with his left hand.

"*A haere!*" ordered Fatu — "Go ahead!"

The diver filled his lungs with air, grinned at us like some goggle-eyed creature of the sea, and let go the gunwale. Coil after coil of line flew over the side, and a train of bubbles rose to the surface, hissing faintly. When the line ceased to run out, Fatu pulled in the slack till it stood taut from the bottom, and made it fast to a cleat. Gazing downward through the water glass, I found that I could see Ofai dimly, in the twilight of the depths. He was swimming close to the bottom, with strange slow motions of his arms and legs; at times he stopped as if examining something, and finally — after what seemed a longer time than any man could hold his breath — I saw him approach the rope, pull himself upright, and heave strongly with one hand. He seemed to shoot upward faster than he had gone down; an instant later his head broke water and he was expelling his breath with the eerie whistling sound I was to know so well. Then he shouted — the long-drawn yodeling cry which announces a lucky dive.

"Never have I seen shell of such a size!" he exclaimed, as he handed up a great coral-encrusted oyster and came clambering over the side. "It grows everywhere — the bottom was covered as far as my eyes could see!"

My uncle was opening the oyster with the blade of his clasp knife. It was a rough, roundish thing, uncouth to the eye, and a full eight inches across. He cut the muscle, felt skillfully but vainly for pearls under the fringe, tossed the soft body overboard, and handed the shells — still attached at the hinge — to me. Craning their necks to see, the natives exclaimed with wonder. When closed, the oyster might have been mistaken for an ugly lump of coral, picked up at random on the floor of the lagoon; when open, it displayed the changing opalescent shades of mother-of-pearl, fringed with a band of gold.

"Get up the anchor," ordered Uncle Harry; "we'll try again, a hundred yards farther on."

"There would be a sensation on Tahiti," he went on, turning to me, "if you showed the trad-

ers that shell! It's worth twenty dollars a ton
more than the black-lipped variety, and the books
say that it produces a great many more pearls.
We'll do a bit of prospecting to-day, mark the
best places, and let the men begin diving in the
morning."

We wandered on for several hours, examining
the bottom at each halt and marking the more
likely spots with a small buoy, moored to the coral
with a few fathoms of line. By mid-afternoon, our
work seemed finished — we had found more shell
than our men could bring up in all the months
ahead of us. Our final halt was close to the reef,
and there, in about ten fathoms of water, Ofai went
overboard for the last time that day.

The coral was light-colored at this place and I
could see every motion of the diver beneath us.
Suddenly, when he had been about a minute under
water, I saw him crouch and disappear in a crevice
of the rock, and an instant later a long moving
shadow passed beneath the boat.

"*E mao!*" exclaimed Fatu. "A shark!" My
uncle sprang to the side.

I leaned over with the rest, watching with acute
suspense to see if the shark would move away. No
— he had seen Ofai and was turning back toward
the deep crevice in which the diver had taken
refuge. Then the shark rose toward us and we saw
him clearly — longer than our boat, livid-brown
and hideous. An exclamation of horror went up
from the men. There seemed nothing we could do.

Thirty seconds passed; Ofai had been under water a minute and a half. My uncle had reached the limit of his endurance. He spoke to Fatu sharply: "Your goggles! That knife! The other weight!"

The shark had approached the surface again, and as he turned to go down, before any of us could utter a cry of protest Uncle Harry went over the side, plunging downward with all the impetus of the heavy leaden bulb. It was an act of the most reckless courage; for in spite of the stories one reads, men do not attack the great sharks of the South Pacific in their own element.

Half sickened with suspense, I watched what followed: a drama played out in the limpid water beneath our boat. Grasping in his right hand a keen broad-bladed knife, my uncle shot down so fast that half-way to the bottom he overtook his monstrous antagonist. The shark was still intent upon Ofai; I saw him start and turn with a sweep of his tail as the man's body struck him and the thrust of a powerful arm sent the knife deep into his side. A pink cloud of blood gushed from the wound, and at that moment I saw Ofai emerge from his hiding-place, seize the rope, and bound toward the surface of the lagoon. The diver's lungs must have been nearly bursting, and he mounted the rope with desperate speed. Now he was close to my uncle. The shark had circled, turning on his side with a livid gleam of his under parts, and was coming straight at the native. The monster reared — again I saw Uncle Harry raise his arm, saw the long knife sink home and the water reddened by a cloud of blood. The respite had been enough for Ofai; his head broke water with a gasp, and before a hand could be raised to help him he had seized the gunwale and was over the side of the boat.

My uncle was in desperate straits. He had been under water nearly a minute and was still eighteen or twenty feet beneath the surface. Fatu and Ivi were brave men and devoted to him, but it would have been insanity to think of going to his rescue now. I heard Fatu's voice, unreal and far-off, shouting to the men to move to the other side of the boat; I felt the boat list, and saw, out of the corner of my eye, the gigantic figure of the mate standing on the seat beside me, bent almost double as he watched the scene below.

Uncle Harry had dropped the weight at the first attack, and now, still grasping his knife, he made for the rope and seized it with his left hand. The shark had darted away as he felt the steel for the second time, but now he was returning straight for the antagonist he seemed to recognize at last. Moving with horrid deliberation, he reared almost vertically beneath the swimmer, and opened his great jaws. My uncle stopped himself with his left hand on the rope, gathered his body together, and drove the knife into the broad rounded snout beneath him — the shark's most vulnerable point. For a moment the monster lay stunned and motionless, and in that moment Uncle Harry nearly reached the surface of the lagoon. Fatu was bent double, his hands already in the water. Then the shark seemed to regain his senses and came rushing upward grimly. I saw the muscles of the mate's arms standing out as though cast in bronze, I saw the swimmer's goggled face within a yard of the surface, and the great fish charging with open jaws, fearfully close behind. Then the whaleboat lurched as Fatu plunged his arms deep into the water, seized my uncle and swung him up and inboard with a single mighty heave.

The shark came crashing against the side of the boat — a blow that nearly stove in the planking and started a dozen seams.

A minute passed before my uncle sat up and lifted the goggles from his eyes. "Get the oars out," he gasped, "and pull for the shallow water yonder. Bale, you two, and look lively — that fellow means mischief!"

The shark was at the surface now, swimming in swift zigzags like a hound at fault. While Ofai and I baled and the others began to row, I glanced over my shoulder and saw the tall dorsal fin heading straight for us, so swiftly that the water rippled away on either side.

"Pull hard — he's after us!" shouted my uncle, standing in the stern with a twelve foot oar in his hand.

We were making for the shallows over a large coral mushroom, a hundred yards away, and the men were rowing at top speed, for they realized that our light cranky boat gave little protection

*The shark reared almost vertically beneath the swimmer
and opened his great jaws.*

against such an enemy. The shark drew rapidly abreast of us and as his head ranged alongside Uncle Harry raised the oar and thrust down with all his strength. The blow was a glancing one, and before he recovered his weapon the three-inch shaft of tough wood was between a pair of formidable jaws. My uncle's eyebrows went up as he raised what was left of the oar, sheared off as a child bites through a stick of candy. Next moment Ivi cried out, as the monster seized his sweep and wrenched it from his hands. I saw it float to the surface with a splintered blade — felt our boat shaken violently as the shark took the keel in his teeth. Then the bow grated on coral, and we leaped out in the shallows to pull the boat into the safety of a foot of water.

After a time the ominous fin tacked away toward the reef and disappeared. We were not anxious for another encounter and allowed our enemy plenty of time to go. The men were talking excitedly in high-pitched voices, when my uncle lit one of his long cigars and turned to me.

"What a brute!" he remarked. "I thought he had me that last time! By Jove! When Fatu took hold of me I could fairly feel those teeth sinking into my legs! Well, our work is cut out for us — there'll be no diving till that fellow is dead. The men are saying that in all probability there are no other dangerous sharks in the lagoon. Do you remember the letter I read you that evening at home? This is the same shark, without a doubt —

he may have been here for a hundred years. He's of a rare kind, by good luck; so rare that I know only his Latin name: *Carcharodon*. They are relics of prehistoric times and seem to be nearly extinct to-day, though a few of them still linger in the warm waters close to the Line. Remember the big fossil teeth, from Florida, on the mantel at the ranch? They came from one of this fellow's ancestors who grew to be ninety feet long and swarmed in the Tertiary seas."

"But won't he die?" I asked. "I saw you stab him three times."

My uncle laughed. "No more than you will," he replied. "A shark of that size takes a lot of killing. But he's going to die to-morrow, if we have to sit up all night hammering out a lance and a harpoon. Our fish-spears would only tickle his ribs. Come, he seems to have given us up — let's be getting back to the Tara."

VI

THE END OF THE SHARK AND
THE BEGINNING OF THE DIVING

THAT Sunday night, while the crew of the Tara told to their friends the story of Ofai's rescue, my uncle and I labored with forge and anvil and grindstone under the shed of corrugated iron. From the schooner's trade-room we took a couple of the whale-spades used throughout the islands as agricultural tools, and removed the wooden hafts from their sockets. While I pumped the bellows, Uncle Harry heated one of these in the forge and hammered it into the shape of a harpoon, welding on a piece of steel to make the socket into which the hinged barb would fit. Then, gripping a morsel of steel in the tongs, he forged out the barb, punched a hole through it, and riveted it in place, so that it folded into its socket when the harpoon was thrown and opened to prevent the iron's withdrawal from the wound. When the harpoon was finished to his satisfaction, I turned the grindstone while he ground it to a razor-edge. After that he heated the other spade and forged out a lance for killing: a slender, double-edged blade, two inches wide and eighteen long — a murderous weapon in skilled hands. We fixed the lance on a twelve-foot pole of hibiscus, and whittled out a short stout shaft for the harpoon, tapered to fit loosely in the socket.

Then my uncle fetched from the storeroom a coil of heavy cotton line. Passing one end of it through a screw eye halfway up the shaft of the harpoon he lashed it firmly to the small of the iron. It was long past midnight.

"We won't get much sleep," he remarked, as we paddled out to the schooner in a canoe. "We must kill that shark to-morrow — to-day, rather —without fail! The natives are superstitious as children; they used to worship sharks, you know, before the missionaries came, and if any ghost-talk starts, we may have to go back for another lot of men. I'll wake you at five o'clock."

I dreamed strange dreams that night, for my mind was feverish with the excitement of the day. I was diving, and like Ofai, I had taken refuge in the coral while a great shark nosed at me from above. But the crevice was too narrow for his head, and I crouched there with bursting lungs, praying that the monster would leave me to reach the air before I drowned. At last I could stand it no longer; I sprang out from my retreat — past the shark gazing at me with fierce green eyes, upward toward the surface, so far off that I gave myself up for lost. The water weighed on me like lead; I seemed to sink instead of rising; I saw the monster approaching, grimly and deliberately. Then he seized my shoulder in his jaws. I felt the sharp teeth tear the flesh and crunch the bone — and I awoke with a strangled shout.

The stateroom was lit by the first gray light of

dawn, and my uncle's hand was on my shoulder as he shook me awake.

"Time for coffee," he said, smiling at my bewildered face. "The men have killed a pig for bait, and they're getting the surfboat ready. We'll be off in half an hour."

We left before sunrise, in the broad heavy boat used for landing cargo from the schooner. I sat aft with Fatu, who held the steering-sweep; Ivi and Ofai pulled, and my uncle stood forward in the bows. The morning was calm, and as we reached the line of buoys we kept a close lookout for the shark, but no fin cut the water and no long shadow passed beneath the boat. Finally, at the place where we had sighted our enemy the day before, we cut open the carcass of the pig, tied it to a buoy, and pulled off a little way to watch.

An hour passed; the sun rose, and the lagoon began to shimmer in the heat. I heard the booming of the breakers where the ring of land was broken north of us and saw the smoke rising vertically from the ovens at our island camp. The natives were half dozing, but my uncle had not relaxed his watch.

"There he is!" he exclaimed suddenly. "Quick — pull over there — don't make a noise with your oars!"

I glanced up as he spoke and saw the dead pig rise and disappear in a circle of ripples. Then the head and forelegs came to the surface again — the carcass of our pig had been bitten in two.

"Row faster," my uncle whispered in the native tongue. "Make haste, or he will eat the pig and go."

Our boat glided toward the feeding monster. Without turning his head, Uncle Harry motioned to the men to cease their rowing, and it was then I caught sight of the huge brownish body of the shark, rising to finish what was left. My uncle brandished the harpoon above his head — hurled it with all the strength of his arm. The water swirled and coil after coil of line flew out through the chock. We were fast.

As he felt the iron, the shark turned with a mighty sweep of his tail and rushed off swiftly to the south. Fatu swung the boat around to follow, and before half the line had streaked overboard we were gathering way. Then my uncle got his hands on the line, paying it out more gradually until our full weight was on the fish; the oars came in and we foamed along at a faster gait, perhaps, than the clumsy surfboat had ever known. The shark seemed tireless — we passed the islet, where the people stood on the beach, waving in answer to our shouts, and sped on toward the southern end of the lagoon. We were following a deep channel in the coral, which turned westward halfway to the pass and approached the long island that formed the atoll's western side. At the end of an hour I could see the village of the copra-makers and the distant pass, a gap in the low ring of wooded land. The channel had brought us close to the inner beach and our pace was slowing appreciably. My uncle was beginning to haul up, when all at once the fish turned at right angles toward the submarine cliff of coral, close at hand. The line went slack; the boat drifted quietly for a few yards, and came to a halt. My uncle turned his head.

"Look," he said, "he's gone into that hole yonder! See the mouth of it a couple of fathoms down? This must be his den."

Holding the line with one hand, he took up the lance and ordered the rowers to back water — to keep a steady galling strain on the fish. "The iron is tickling him," he remarked when five minutes had passed. "I can feel him twitch. Look lively now! He'll be out in a moment — Ah! Here he comes!"

Far in beneath the coral the cave must have broadened, for the shark had turned to face the entrance of his lair. He came out with a rush, maddened by the pain of his wound, open-mouthed and at bay. Before Ofai could pull in his oar the monster had wrenched it from his hands and turned to sink his teeth in the cutwater of the boat. But my uncle was ready with the lance. Again and again his arm rose and thrust downward, and at each stroke the keen blade bit deep. The water reddened; the jaws relaxed their hold; the tail ceased its lashing and lay quiet. The huge carcass turned belly-upward and sank in the clear blue channel beneath us.

Uncle Harry laid down the lance and came aft to light a cigar. "That's a good day's work," he said. "No diving with that fellow about! He's sinking

now; we'll have the boys cut the line and make
the end fast to the coral. To-morrow he'll float high
— I'll send a couple of men to cut out the jaws.
They'll make you a fine souvenir of Iriatai."

There was rejoicing when we arrived at camp,
for the native regards a large shark with a peculiar,
superstitious dread. There had been much talk
among the divers since the night before, but now
their fears were at an end and they busied themselves with preparations for the ensuing day.

That night, when dinner was over and we sat
talking on the Tara's deck, my uncle explained
to me the terms of the agreement under which his
divers worked. "Ordinarily," he said, "when the
Government opens the lagoons the men are free
to keep everything they bring up: the shell and
the pearls are theirs to do with as they please.
The traders keep track of all the better men and
do their best to get them as deeply as possible in
debt before the season begins. You can imagine
what happens when credit is offered to simple fellows like these Paumotans: they run up bills for
all sorts of useless trash — guitars; silk dresses and
high-heeled shoes for their women; cheap perfume
at five or six dollars a bottle; every kind of fancy
white-man's food in tins. They load up with this
sort of stuff till they are over their heads in debt.
By the time he begins to dive, each native is safe in
the clutches of some trading-house — Chinese, more
often than not — and every pearl and every pound of
shell must be sold to the creditor at the creditor's price.

"It is different here on Iriatai, for the men know that I have a year's monopoly of the lagoon. But there is more shell, and it lies in shallower water than in the lagoons which have been worked for a generation, so the divers are glad to accept my terms. Ever since I came to the islands I have tried to deal honestly with the people, for I have a theory that the savage appreciates a square deal as well as a civilized man. It has paid me, too. As you know, I am furnishing the canoes and advancing a reasonable amount of food and goods. The men have agreed, on their side, to work every day the weather permits and to let me make the first offer on their catch. Half of the shell goes to me; all of the pearls and the other half of the shell will be theirs. At the end of the season I'll make each man an offer on his shell — cleaned, sacked, and loaded aboard the Tara. As for the pearls, they will be brought out every night and offered for sale to me. Those I do not care to buy, or for which the owners think they can get a higher price in Tahiti, will be sold in the open market when we go North. But I'll get all the really fine ones — I can pay good prices and still double my money in every case!"

In the morning I had my first sight of pearl-diving as it is practised among the atolls of the Paumotus.

The men we had brought with us from Raiatea, reënforced by a few volunteers from the copra-makers of Iriatai, made up fifteen crews of two men

each. I say men, but one of the best of the lot was
an elderly brown woman, and there was not a man
who could dive deeper than old Maruia, or bring
up more shell in a day.

Each canoe was equipped with its paddles, an
anchor at the end of thirty fathoms of line, a five-
gallon kerosene-tin, a stout knife, and two coils of
light rope — one attached to the diving-weight,
the other to a large openwork basket of bamboo.
The two members of the crew shared equally in the
catch, though almost without exception one man
did all the diving while his partner remained at
the surface, raising and lowering the basket, cleaning the shell roughly, opening the oysters and
inspecting them for pearls.

As they worked no more than five hours a day,
we did not leave camp till the sun was well up,
illuminating the bottom of the lagoon. I went out
with a pair of middle-aged Paumotans whose
acquaintance I had made during the passage from
Raiatea. It was about half a mile from the islet
to the patch of shell on which work was to begin.
Uncle Harry had gone out ahead of us in the whaleboat and as the little fleet of canoes drew near, he
pointed out to the paddlers the two acres of lagoon
in which they were to work. The bow-man in our
canoe dropped anchor in about seventy feet of
water, and began to prepare himself to dive.

First of all, he stripped off the cotton shirt he
had been wearing and hitched the pareu tight about
his waist. Then he polished his water goggles,

adjusted them carefully over his eyes, and thrust his right hand into a heavy working-glove. A pile of coral lumps, picked up on the beach the night before, lay in the bottom of the canoe; the stern-man placed a couple of these in the basket and lowered it into the lagoon till it came to rest on the bottom. Then the diver went over the side and lay in the water with a hand on the gunwale of the canoe, while his partner coiled the diving-line and lowered the leaden weight till it hung a few feet beneath the surface. The man in the water gripped the line with his left hand and the toes of his left foot; he took two or three long breaths before he jerked his head upward in a sudden gesture that meant: "Let go!" Coil after coil of line went leaping overboard, as the diver sank like a stone, leaving a trail of bubbles in his wake. When the lead touched bottom the stern-man hauled it up at once, coiling the line in readiness for the next dive.

A minute passed — a minute and a quarter — a minute and a half. The canoe lurched to a sudden strain on the taut basket-line. I looked over the side. Far down in the green water I could see the shadowy figure of the diver, mounting the rope with leisurely movements of his arms. He came to the surface, exhaling the breath from his lungs with the strange shrill whistle I had heard before. Then, raising the goggles from his eyes, he gave the exultant whoop of the diver who has brought up a rich haul — a cry that was beginning to ring out on all sides, where the canoes lay at anchor.

He lay resting alongside while his companion pulled up the basket, loaded with six or seven great gold-lipped oysters; and craned his neck to watch as the other opened the shells with a twist of his knife at the hinge, felt for pearls under the soft mantle, and tossed the body of each mollusk into the open kerosene-tin. My companions seemed excited.

"*Aué!*" exclaimed the diver. "There is no other island like this! It is as Seroni told us — the bottom is covered with shell, and the water is not overdeep: twelve fathoms, by the knots on my line. Last year, at Hikueru, I worked at twenty till my head ached all through the night. And this shell — the size, the weight, the color of the lip — think of what it must be worth a ton! No man in all these islands has ever seen its like! I would still dive if there were fifty sharks instead of the one Seroni killed yesterday. But watch carefully, and if a shark comes, move the basket up and down a little so that I may be warned. Now pass me the weight, for I am ready to go down again."

At the end of three hours the diver clambered stiffly into the canoe; even in this water, only a few degrees below the temperature of one's blood, a man grows chilled and must come out to rest and warm himself in the sun. He had averaged a minute and a half to two minutes under water, and five minutes' rest at the surface between dives, and I noticed that he sent up five or six oysters each time he went down. We had brought along a bottle of water and a package of cold food done up in leaves. When lunch was over and the diver lay basking in the sun, I asked him how he could stay under water so long, and how a man could stand the pressure of the depths. At home in California I had excelled my friends by bringing up sand from the bottom at thirty feet, and my ears had ached for an hour afterward. These natives thought nothing of working at seventy feet, and from what they said, I knew that one hundred and twenty feet was not considered an extraordinary depth.

"It is not difficult," the diver remarked, smiling at my efforts to question him in his own tongue. "If he would take the trouble, the white man could learn as well as we. But one must know how. You say that at six fathoms your head ached and your lungs were bursting. That was because you tired yourself by swimming down instead of letting a weight pull you to the bottom. And perhaps you held all of your breath until you rose — that is wrong. First of all, you must learn never to tire yourself beneath the water, and not to fill your lungs too full before you start. When your time is half up, you must begin to let the air out of your lungs, little by little, — a few bubbles now and then, — so that, as you reach the top, there will be scarcely any air left in you. If your ears ache, swallow; or hold your nose and blow — this will clear the little passages between your nose and ears, and stop the pain. That is all, except that in deep water you must never look up, nor bend your body backward. As for the sharks, there is little

danger — not one in a hundred will do you harm.
When that one comes, you will know him by the
way he swims, and if there is sand or mud on the
bottom, you can escape by throwing it up to cloud
the water while you pull yourself quickly up the
basket-rope. Otherwise you can only take refuge
in a crevice of the coral, hoping that the shark will
leave you before your lungs go flat. Conger eels
are more to be feared; you must watch sharply as
you pass the holes where they lie hidden. The big
eel's jaws are like the jaws of a dog! If a conger
seizes wrist or ankle, it is useless to struggle — ten
strong men could not drag one from his hole. Three
times, when I was young and careless, I have felt
the teeth of the eel; see — my ankles bear the scars
to this day. But I remembered what the old men
had told me and lay quietly without struggling,
till the conger relaxed his jaws to dart forward for
a better hold. Each time I tore my ankle free and
reached the surface with only the loss of a little
blood. But we must get to work — the others are
beginning to dive."

The canoes returned to camp in mid-afternoon.
The women were waiting to begin their task of
cleaning shell, and there were exclamations of wonder as the day's catch was brought ashore. While
the men went off to rest, their wives and daughters
sat gossiping in little groups, hammering, chipping,
and washing the mother-of-pearl. Half of the catch
of each canoe had been set aside as my uncle's
share, and some of his own people — Ivi, Ofai, and

a few men and women from the settlement on
Iriatai — set to work to clean it in a space reserved
for them. I saw a number of women along the
beach, filling the tins from the canoes with sea
water, mashing the soft meat between their fingers,
and pouring off the mess little by little, as they
searched for any pearls that might have been
overlooked. My uncle was delighted with the first
day's work.

"It is going better than I had hoped," he said,
as we sat in his stateroom that evening. "They
brought in about two tons of shell to-day, and the
quality is superb — nothing like it has ever been
seen in this part of the Pacific. Your canoe had no
luck, but the others netted four handsome pearls
and a number of small ones for the day. That
alone proves that there must be something in von
Tesmar's theory. I've seen thousands of black-
lipped oysters opened without a pearl. Old Maruia
found a beauty to-day, with her usual luck. I gave
her a thousand dollars for it, and any jeweler in
Paris would jump at a chance to offer twice as much.
You are smiling, eh, to think of that funny old
woman having a thousand dollars, all at once?
Why, in the eyes of her people Maruia is a million-
aire! Twenty years of diving have made her the
owner of a fine plantation, and one of the pretti-
est villas on Tahiti. Ah — I almost forgot to show
you our first pearls."

He leaned over to twirl the knob of the safe,
swung open the door, and took from the shelf a

small tobacco-tin, which he opened and handed to me. It was lined with cotton and there, lying side by side like tiny eggs in a nest, were four pearls, pale, lustrous, and without a flaw. Three of them were like peas in size and the other was larger than the three together, — I had never seen a pearl of such size and beauty, — shimmering with a soft opalescence in its bed. My uncle took it in his hand, turning it to admire the perfection of its shape.

"You won't see a pearl like this five times in a season," he remarked. "There are many larger ones of greater value, but there is nearly always something wrong with them — a flattened spot, a flaw on the surface, a dullness in orient. Though not of great size, this is a really perfect pearl. If I had a mate for it I could ask my own price for the pair!

"I wish now that I had brought a few more men," he went on, "but I think we can make out by shutting down the copra-making and putting everyone at work. I am going to put Fatu and Ofai to diving, with a couple of stern-men from the village; they say we can find trees to build two or three more canoes. The others will have to work at cleaning shell, and from now on I'm counting on you and Marama to feed us. Tins are all right in an emergency, but it would be absurd to make ourselves ill on canned stuff in a place swarming with excellent fish. There are eight of us on board, counting the new cook, and I want you to supply us with fish. You can begin to-morrow — I'll give you the small canoe and whatever gear you need."

VII

SOUTH SEA FISHERMEN

I HAVE always loved fishing since I was old enough
to hold a rod and cast out into the surf at home,
and now, as I look back on the months spent with
my uncle in the South Seas, I know that my happiest memories of Iriatai are of the long hours in a
canoe with Marama in the lagoon or on the open
sea beyond the reef. It was fishing in unspoiled
waters — fishing to dream about in after years.
Our primitive tackle, much of which was fashioned
by our own hands, did not detract from the charm
of the sport, and the background — the land, the
sea, the sky — was hauntingly and strangely
beautiful.

Some of those nights were unforgettable — calm
nights when we lay off the reef from sunset till
dawn began to brighten in the east. In all that solitude our lantern was the only light, the only sign of
man. Iriatai lay like a shadow on the sea, stretching off vaguely to the south, and the heavens above
us were powdered with stars of a brilliance I had
never known before. The native boy was a better
astronomer than I; he had names for many of the
constellations, and strange old stories to tell of
them. Castor and Pollux, the Twins, sinking on
the horizon to the west, he called *Pipiri-Ma* — a
boy and a girl, he told me, who had lived in very

ancient times and who, because of their unkind
parents, had fled away to the skies. The Southern
Cross was *Tatauro;* the Scorpion was a great fishhook, flung into the sky after a god had used it to
pull up the islands of the Paumotus; the Pleiades,
visible in the east an hour before the dawn, he called
Matarii — the Little Eyes, and told me a pretty
story of their origin.

Much of our fishing was done at night, when we
fished offshore for the great bottom-feeders of the
South Pacific: the deep-water albicore, the castor-
oil fish, and the *manga* — a long black creature
shaped like an enormous pickerel, with goggle-
eyes and rows of formidable teeth.

Our custom was to start an hour before sunset
and paddle north to a break between the two long
islands, where we dragged our canoe through the
ankle-deep wash of the barrier, waited our moment,
and slipped out through the surf. The outer face
of the reef shelved off steeply, and our line, which
reached the bottom at two hundred fathoms, would
have reached the reef as well. Marama usually
took the stern, paddling gently, while I did the
fishing forward. Our bait was fish, saved from the
previous day's catch and salted. I chose a morsel
large as a man's fist and tied it with strong thread
to the point of one of the great wooden hooks used
in this deep-sea fishing: a fork of ironwood, six
inches from tip to tip, and barbed with a cod-hook
lashed on to point down and inward. It was useless,
I learned, to fish with an ordinary hook for these

dwellers on the bottom. Their habit of swimming down vertically, to seize the bait from above, made necessary the use of our barbaric implement. When my hook was baited, I fastened a large pebble to the line, with a special hitch that Marama had taught me. Coil after coil ran out as the pebble sank, until at last I felt the slackening which told me that it had touched bottom. Hauling up a yard or two, I gave the jerk which freed my coral sinker, and settled myself to wait. Sometimes an hour passed without a strike, and then, when I was least prepared for it, some monster of a hundred pounds seized my hook with a rush that carried my arm elbow-deep into the black water alongside. Hand over hand I brought him slowly to the surface till he lay wallowing beside the canoe, eyes bulging with the release from the pressure of his deep-sea haunts. A blow with the blunt side of our whale-spade ended his struggles, and taking hold by the gills, we tilted the canoe and slid the quivering body inboard.

Sometimes, as my fish neared the surface, I felt a sudden slackening of the line — one of the small sharks that prowled along the reef at night had helped himself, leaving only a bodiless and gaping head upon the hook. Once or twice, when the marauder rose close to our canoe, Marama sprang to his feet in a rage — keen-bladed spade in hand — and ended the shark's life with a cutting blow forward of the eyes. At those times we seized our paddles and made off swiftly for new fishing-grounds; for the scene of the ensuing feast was no place for our light canoe.

Fishing by night meant sleeping through the warm hours of the day. Sometimes, when we wearied of this, the order was reversed and we went out at daybreak to pursue the schools of bonito far offshore. The lures for bonito are made of mother-of-pearl, and the fisherman must carry six or seven different shades to suit the varying conditions of sea and sky. Marama selected half a dozen large pearl-shells, shading from light to dark, and marked with a pencil on the thickest part of each the outline of a small fish. When this was done we took our shell to the shop my uncle had set up ashore, and set to work with vise and hacksaw to cut out the lures. Then came the grinding and polishing, and finally a barbless hook of brass was attached to each, the line made fast to the forward end, and a tuft of coconut fibre bound on across the rear. We tied the lines to a stiff pole of bamboo, ten or twelve feet long and equipped with a ring at the butt end, in which to hook the lures when not in use.

Bonito-fishing was hard work and not unspiced with danger, — the risk of being swamped or blown offshore in a squall, — but it had a fascination of its own. We used to paddle half a mile out to sea and wait in the morning calm, on the lookout for birds. At sunrise the boobies and noddy terns left their roosting-places by hundreds and cruised about over the sea, singly or in little bands, in search of breakfast. We watched them flying this way and that until at last, perhaps a mile away, a dozen noddies began to circle and dive. Then it was time to seize our paddles and strain our backs to make for the birds at top speed. Keener eyes than ours had been on the watch, and before a minute had passed hungry sea-birds were flapping from all directions toward the school of fish. The small fish, pursued by both bonito and birds, were far from remaining stationary; sometimes they sounded and disappeared altogether; sometimes, when our backs were aching with an hour's chase, they swept off to windward at a pace that made us lay down our paddles in despair. There were days when we went home worn out and empty-handed, but there were other days when luck was with us and we drove the canoe into the midst of ravenous schools. Then, while the man forward paddled with all his might, the stern-man faced about, long rod in hand and lure skittering over the waves behind us. A hasty trial proved which shade of mother-of-pearl was most attractive, and next moment fish after fish came tumbling aboard — fat, steel-blue, and vibrant. There were days when we hooked and landed thirty fish in half as many minutes, before we sank down exhausted to rest, leaving the birds to circle off above the foaming sea.

Sometimes, when we could get bait, we enjoyed a sport even more thrilling than bonito-fishing — trolling along the reef at daybreak for tunny, barracuda, and the giant cavally of the Pacific. A silvery species of mullet proved the best lure for the fish that lay in wait in the caverns along the outer edge of the reef, and many of our afternoons were spent in mullet-catching. First of all we prepared a mass of paste, made of flour or arrowroot, and with this for bait, we paddled to a place in the lagoon where the water shoaled to three or four feet over a coral bottom. Our tackle was a stick of light wood eighteen inches long, attached by a trace to twenty feet of line, and fitted with a small hook on a leader at either end. One of us baited the hooks with bits of paste and stood ready to cast the stick, while the other threw pieces of our dough ahead of the motionless canoe. Presently the water would dimple and swirl with rising mullet — it was time to cast. The float lay quietly for a moment — bobbed — jerked — disappeared under water, with a pair of fat mullet, as often as not, fast on the hooks. We kept them alive in an openwork basket floating alongside, and towed our catch back to the Tara, in readiness for the morning's fishing.

An hour before sunrise we dragged our canoe over the reef, shot out through the breakers, and paddled to our favorite trolling-grounds — a shoal which ran out a quarter of a mile to sea. Our hook for this kind of fishing was equipped with a leader of piano-wire, which was passed lengthwise through the body of a mullet and pulled through the mouth until the shank of the hook was out of sight. Then the lips were lashed to the wire with a bit of thread and the leader made fast to the end of a hundred yards of heavy line. Arranged in this way and towed at a good pace behind the canoe, the mullet flashed and zigzagged through the water in imitation of a living fish — an imitation so perfect that many a wary old dweller on the reef was deceived and came rushing upward to his death.

The handling of these powerful fish required all our skill, and Marama, being more experienced than I, usually took the stern on trolling-expeditions. Making the line fast to the outrigger-pole which crossed the canoe behind his seat, he gave the word, and we began to paddle our hardest, following the edge of the shoal. As the sun rose, one could look down and see the changing colors of the coral — every fold and crevice clearly visible ten fathoms beneath us. There were certain crannies and caverns where we knew the big fish lay, and as we passed above them we increased our efforts to make speed. In this kind of sport there was no holding the line to feel for a bite; we were never in doubt when a monster tunny or barracuda struck. The canoe quivered with the shock. Sometimes we fought for half an hour while the hooked fish towed us in rushes, this way and that. One old barracuda, I remember, — seven feet long and with the jaws of a shark, — pulled us more than a mile before he lay exhausted at the surface.

We seldom returned from trolling till the trade wind came up at eight or nine o'clock, for a good catch, sufficient for two or three days, meant rest and time for other amusements. The weather was hot of course, and we had no ice, but the native method of cooking — baking over and over again, which improves the flavor with each succeeding day — permitted fish to be kept for as long as a week. On days of leisure we rested, overhauled our tackle, or went in search of the shellfish which abounded at Iriatai.

There were lobsters, crabs, and sea snails on the reef, clams and mussels in the lagoon, and best of all, — to be found on patches of shallow sandy bottom, — there were *varos*, creatures whose repulsive English name is "sea centipede." They look like the tail of a lobster, with rows of legs along the sides and a small head, armed with a pair of wicked nippers, said to inflict a poisoned wound. The varo is no beauty, but if it is broiled over a charcoal fire and eaten hot with melted butter, I agreed with my uncle that the sea produced nothing half so good.

One calm morning, when there was a plentiful supply of fish aboard, Marama suggested that we try our luck at varo-fishing and showed me the tackle he had made the afternoon before. It consisted of half a dozen slender sticks of wood to which rows of small fishhooks were lashed, points out. Each stick was provided with a few feet of line and a light float, made fast to the upper end. While I was examining these curious snares, my uncle passed along the deck and stopped at sight of us.

"Going after varos, eh?" he remarked. "The men used to say there were plenty of them here. Good luck to you — we'll have a feast here tonight if you can get some!"

The native boy threw his snares and a few pieces of smelly fish into our canoe and we paddled to the western shore of the lagoon, where a bottom of mud and sand ran out from shore. He allowed the canoe to drift over the shoal while he scanned the bottom through the calm water, clear as glass. Here and there I saw that the sand was pitted with holes, the burrows of various marine creatures; and presently Marama pointed down to one, smaller than the rest and surrounded by a little mound of sand. "That is the dwelling of the varo," he said, "I can tell by its freshness and the smallness of the opening that he is at home."

I held the canoe in place while he took up one of the snares, tied a bit of fish to the upper end, and unwound the short line attached to the float. Then he tucked up his pareu and went overboard. Taking a long breath and working with head and shoulders submerged, he enlarged the mouth of the burrow until its full size was exposed and inserted the baited stick — gently, so as not to alarm the creature inside. Varos were plentiful at this place; we set all our snares within a radius of fifty yards and sat at leisure in the canoe, watching the floats for the first signs of life. We had not long to wait; Marama pointed to one of the floats which was beginning to bob and twitch; a few strokes of the paddle brought us alongside and he went overboard again.

The fishhooks on the snares were lashed on in tiers of three, pointing out and up. The bait was

tied to the upper half of the stick, so that in order to
get at it, the varo was obliged to pass the uppermost
tier of hooks. As it tore the fish with its nippers
and crammed the pieces into its mouth, its hard
back was against the wall of the burrow and its
more vulnerable under-parts in range of the barbs.
Marama put his head under water again, seized the
end of the stick and held the varo against the side
of its hole; then, with a quick pull, he sank his
hooks into the creature's under joints and held up
the snare with a triumphant shout, the captive
struggling and waving its claws. "Take care you
are not hurt," he told me as he broke off the nippers. "They cut like scissors and they are poisoned
— the wounds will fester and swell for weeks!"

At ten o'clock, when the breeze came up, we paddled back to the schooner with a score of varos in
the bottom of our canoe, a feast for all hands.

As we crossed the lagoon Marama spoke to me
suddenly at the end of a long silence. "Listen,
Tehare," he said, — "Tehare" was as near as he
could come to pronouncing my name, — "let us
speak together, for there is a plan in my mind. I
dare not ask Seroni myself. Fishing is the work he
gave me, but he is your father's brother and if you
desire to do the thing that I propose, perhaps you
will speak to him. You have learned much about
our fishing and you see how easy it is to provide for
the Tara's needs: two or three nights each week
give us more fish than we can use. It is in my mind
that on days when there is fish in plenty we might

take this canoe and go out with the others to dive. I can dive deeper than one need go in this lagoon, and you can pull up the basket and open shell, since men are not accustomed to diving in your land. We shall get much shell, and perhaps a great pearl like the one Maruia found. What say you — will you ask Seroni?"

VIII

I TURN PEARL–DIVER

MY chance came the same afternoon, as we were finishing lunch. At last Uncle Harry lit a cigar and called for coffee. "By Jove!" he remarked as he blew out a cloud of fragrant smoke, "those varos were wonderfully good. I reckon the best restaurant in San Francisco could n't produce a finer dish!" The moment seemed opportune.

"We can always get plenty when the weather is calm," I said, "in fact it only takes a third of our time to catch more fish than the Tara can use. We were speaking of this to-day and wondering if you would n't let us go out with the divers in our spare time; Marama says he has often been down to twelve fathoms, and offers to do the diving if I will open shell. I wish you could let us go — it would be fun and somehow I feel sure that we'd be lucky. Of course, if you'd let me, I'd like to try a little diving myself." My uncle looked at me with a twinkle in his dark eyes.

"I knew you'd ask me that sooner or later," he said. "As a matter of fact I ought not to let you do it — I'm responsible to your father, after all, and old Taura's a good friend of mine. Diving is always a dangerous business, though I don't believe there are any more bad sharks in the lagoon. Still, the other men do it every day, and you two are old enough to take the same risks. If I had youngsters of my own, they'd have to take their chances with the rest — otherwise they'd miss their share of good times and hard knocks, and become the helpless sort of men and women who are no use in the world. Yes, you may go, and dive too, if you wish. But, for my sake, keep your eyes open and be as careful as you can!"

That evening, when the day's work was over and the people lay on mats before their houses, smoking and gossiping in the brief twilight, we went ashore. My uncle led the way to where old Maruia lived with one of her nephews: Teura, a pleasant and amusing boy, who paddled her canoe to the diving-grounds and opened the shell that she brought up. Her house was surrounded by a fence of stakes, inside which a pair of pigs wandered, rooting up the earth. As we opened the gate, I heard her voice give the hospitable shout of *"Haere mai! —* Come in!"

"I have come to talk with you about Tehare, my nephew," said Uncle Harry, when a mat had been spread and we had taken our places on it, native-fashion. "He and Marama have become so clever at the sea fishing that we are glutted with fish and time hangs heavy on their hands. To-day they have asked me if they might go out and dive for shell with you others; they are strong boys and well grown — it is in my mind to let them go. What think you of the plan? Is Iriatai a lagoon overdangerous for boys?"

The old woman shook her head as she replied.
"There is little danger here," she said. "Ten
fathoms would not hurt a child, and the great shark
you killed was the only evil shark in the lagoon.
And he was not a shark, as I and all the others
know! For the rest, we have seen neither *tonu* nor
conger eel in all the days we have been diving,
though it is well to watch closely, for a tonu is an
ill thing to meet! But let them go — they will
come to no harm; perhaps they will find a pearl
like mine, and in any case the white boy will have
strange tales to tell when he returns to his own land.
I myself will show them where there is shell in seven
fathoms of water — not so much as where we dive,
but a good place to begin. Let them beware of the
clefts and crevices where an eel might lurk, and
avoid the dark caverns in the coral, for it is in such
places that the tonu lies in wait. There seems little
to fear in Iriatai, but one is never sure. As for
pearls, watch always for the great lone oysters
crusted with coral and misshapen with old age —
parau tahito, we call them, and every diver knows
that they contain the finest pearls."

When the divers went out next morning Marama
and I went with them, our canoe equipped like the
others with basket and weight and line. Maruia,
smoking a cigarette in the bow of her canoe while
Teura paddled, showed us the way to a patch of
shell she had found in shallow water, a quarter of a
mile east of where the others were diving. "Drop
your anchor here," she said, bending over the gun-

wale to examine the bottom. "The depth is seven
fathoms and there is enough shell to keep you busy,
though not so much nor of such great size as in the
deeper water where we work. Now I must leave —
stay here, you two!"

I weighted the basket with a heavy stone and lowered it till it rested on the bottom, while Marama
tucked up his pareu, adjusted his goggles, and
fastened the glove on his right hand. Then he went
overboard, a grin on his brown good-natured face.
I passed him the weight; at the signal, I let go the
line and watched him shoot down into the blue and
green of the depths. After all, seven fathoms were
more than forty feet. I pulled up the lead, coiled
the line for the next dive, and waited, watching the
figure of my companion, seen dimly in the twilight
beneath the canoe, as he moved along the bottom
with deliberate motions of the arms and legs. Once
I thought I saw him place something in the basket,
and finally, when more than two minutes had
elapsed, he seized the upright line and pulled himself to the surface. But he gave no shout of exultation as he raised the goggles from his eyes.

"Aué!" he exclaimed, shaking his head, "it is
more difficult than I had thought! The oysters are
there, but I have not the eyes to see them, nor the
art to twist them off the rocks. There is no need to
pull up the basket; I got only two oysters, though
in all my life I have never stayed longer beneath the
water. But I shall learn!"

All through that morning Marama dove with

increasing success. It was well for me that he did
not send up as much shell as the older divers, for I
was clumsy at opening it and so afraid of missing
a pearl that I wasted a great deal of time in useless
fumbling under the fringes of the oysters. At midday I had found no pearls, but the shell Marama
had brought up was opened and neatly stacked
amidships, and the soft bodies of the oysters were
thrown into our kerosene-tin for inspection in the
evening.

"I am going to dive this afternoon," I announced
to Marama, as we lay resting after lunch.

"That is well," he answered. "I am not accustomed to being so long in the water — my bones are
chilled! I will open the shell and you can try your
hand as I have done. It is strange down there, and
very beautiful, with the coral colored like flowers
and the great fish passing close at hand. At first I
was a little afraid. Do not let yourself grow discouraged; the shell is hard to see and harder still to
wrench off until you learn the trick. Remember
that the old divers never look upward — to gaze
into the blue water overhead gives one a horror of
the depth!"

At last, with a beating heart, I made ready for
my first dive. I loved the sun, which had burned
my back and shoulders to the color of mahogany,
and I wore nothing but a pareu. This savage garment I hitched about my waist as I had seen the
others do, before I polished my glasses and fastened
the glove tightly on my wrist. Once in the water,

I held the lead-line with my left hand and the toes of my left foot, adjusted the goggles to my eyes and gave the signal to let go. I saw Marama's answering grin — felt the water close over my head. Then, gripping the line tightly, I plunged down into a strange purple twilight.

An instant later there was a gentle shock and the line slackened in my hand. I had reached the bottom. My ears ached and the pressure on my chest and stomach made my body feel as if it were being squeezed flat. I could understand now the curiously deliberate movements of the divers, for my limbs seemed weighted with lead — the same feeling I have had in dreams, when to my horror I have found myself unable to avoid the attack of some nightmare monster. I swallowed as I had been instructed, then held my nose and blew. The pains in my head ceased at once.

Frightened and ill at ease, I let go the line and saw the weight ascending through the deep bluish purple of the sea above me, which seemed, like the earth's atmosphere, to extend upward into infinity. There was no sign of the surface — nothing to catch the eye in the break between sea and air. For a moment I was in a panic; it seemed to me that I should never reach the air again, never feel the friendly warmth of the sun nor see the bright sun-lit world above. Then I saw the bottom of the canoe, close over my head. Fifteen or twenty seconds had passed, and though far from feeling at home, I had gained enough assurance to gaze with interest at the strange new world in which I found myself.

Though not so dark as the greater depths I visited later on, there was far less light than I had supposed. The floor of the lagoon, here at seven fathoms, was bathed in a sort of purplish twilight which enabled me to see as clearly, I should say, as on an average moonlight night ashore. But instead of being silvery, like moonlight, the light was purple, and tinged with changing shades of green and blue. The bottom was of dense reef-coral, which dies when sheltered from the breaking sea, but a hundred fantastic varieties of still-water coral grew on the dead madrepore, as vegetation grows on the inanimate earth, and its forms were those of vegetation. Close beneath me I saw little coral plants, fragile as violets or anemones; on a level with my head were leafless shrubs, marvelously colored and perfect in trunk and limb and twig; yonder a giant mushroom, ten feet across and growing on a tall thick stalk, towered above the undergrowth. Shoals of small fish, gay as the bird life of the tropics, drifted through the coral foliage or darted into the shelter of the mushrooms when larger fish passed overhead.

The floor of the lagoon was irregular, seamed by gullies and rising in rough hillocks here and there, and my weighted basket lay at the edge of one of these ravines. By swimming slowly in a horizontal position I could move from place to place without great effort, and hoping to find at least one oyster

before I was forced to rise for air, I swam along the
brink, scanning the coral sharply for the pearl
oysters I knew to be plentiful at this place. A great
silver cavally, four feet long and with goggle-eyes
as large as dollars, darted out of a gloomy cleft,
halted to gaze at me for an instant, passed within a
foot of my face, and disappeared in the shadows.
The fish gave me a start; in the flurry I let go a
good half of my breath, which rose in a string of
bubbles toward the air. My lungs were cramped.
I had reached the limit of endurance.

I made for the line, seized it with both hands,
heaved strongly and felt myself bounding upward
like a cork. When my head broke water and I
raised the goggles from my eyes, I saw that the
native boy was bending over me with an air of
concern.

"Another moment," he said, "and I would have
gone down after you. You were long on the bottom
— I feared that you had been seized with cramps."

"It is strange down there," I answered, a little
apologetically, "the pressure — the dim light — I
was so interested that I nearly forgot to look for
shell and when I did look there was none to be seen."

"It was the same with me at first," declared
Marama, smiling, "but if you look closely in the
rough places, on piles of coral and along the edges
of the gullies, you will see the oysters there by
hundreds. It is easy to mistake them for lumps of
rock — coral and barnacles grow on them as on
the rock itself. They lie open like the *pahua* (the

tridacna clam), but that helps you little, for their fringes are not blue and yellow like the clam's tongue."

I did not waste my strength by climbing into the canoe, but lay in the water resting as I had seen the natives do. When five minutes had passed I put down my glasses and went to the bottom again, and this time I saw two pearl-oysters. I found them at the edge of the gulley, when I was on the point of giving up in despair of seeing the elusive things. They looked for all the world like irregular lumps of coral, projecting like hundreds of other lumps from the rocky wall, and I would have passed without a second glance if one of them had not moved. Though they have no eyes, in our sense of the word, all bivalves which do not habitually lie buried in sand or mud seem to possess a subtle sense of light. As my body passed over the oyster, shutting off the light, the creature was thus mysteriously warned, and instantly its shells closed with a smooth swiftness. Looking more closely, I recognized the outlines of the *margaritifera*, the pearl oyster, beneath a protective growth of parasites, and grasping it with my gloved hand, I endeavored to wrench it from its fibrous moorings. As I struggled to free it from the coral, the water must have been agitated, for another rough lump closed with the same smooth swift movement, revealing a second great oyster. By this time I had been under nearly a minute, and though I tugged with all my might I was unable to wrench the shell free before I rose.

"I have seen the oysters," I told Marama, as I lay resting in the sunlight, "but try as I would, I could not tear one loose!"

He picked up an opened shell from the bottom of the canoe.

"Take hold thus," he instructed me, "and turn the oyster with a sudden wrench. It is useless to pull. Ah — your left hand is bleeding — take care to use the gloved hand only, for the coral cuts like a knife, and oftentimes the wounds are poisoned."

By the third time down I had gained confidence and was beginning to feel at home on the bottom. Now I remembered the trick of which the Paumotan diver had told me, and when I had been half a minute under water I began to let the air out of my lungs. The native had spoken truly; each little string of bubbles brought its moment of relief and enabled me to go about my work more calmly.

I was beginning to see the oysters now: my eyes were growing accustomed to the dim light. This time I managed to tear off a couple of oysters and put them in the basket before I rose for air. Three dives filled the basket, and when Marama pulled it from the water with its coral-encrusted load, I gave an imitation of the exultant native shout — a cry which brought a grin to my companion's face.

"We are learning," he said mockingly, "but it will be time to shout when we can fill the basket at one dive!"

That afternoon, when we joined the little fleet of canoes to paddle home, Maruia stood up, craning her neck for a look at our catch. "You have done well," she remarked, a smile wrinkling her brown face, "not badly for the first day's diving! I have seen grown men do worse. No pearls? Never mind — you will find them surely. Beginners always have the luck!"

From that day onward the fishing occupied less than a third of our time, and the balance was put in on the lagoon. We learned fast, as boys do, and gradually worked our way into deeper water till we were diving with the rest. Within a few weeks we were bringing in as much shell as the Paumotans, and my uncle was enthusiastic over our success. He could dive with any native, and once or twice, when he had leisure, he sent Marama out alone to fish and accompanied me to the diving-grounds. On those days my uncle's share of the shell went to the native boy's account — growing into a round little sum.

As for me, the diving fascinated me more each day: the beauty and strangeness of the underwater world; the spice of danger — small, but a reality, nevertheless; the thought of the money I was earning; the daily, even hourly, hope of finding a rich pearl, perhaps worth a small fortune. From time to time we found a few small pearls, but when at last good fortune came to us, it came hand in hand with tragedy.

As the nearer shell-patches became worked out, the canoes moved gradually northward, taking the cream of the shell without diving enough to exhaust the beds at any one place. One morning, in the latter part of July, Marama and I anchored close beside Maruia's canoe, on new and very promising grounds. It was my turn to open shell. The Paumotan woman, not ten yards away from me, was loafing that day — letting her nephew dive, for once. Teura was a boy of twenty or twenty-one, a favorite among the natives because of his skill as a musician and his jokes. I had grown fond of him since we had been thrown with the divers, and often went ashore in the evening to chat with old Maruia and listen to her nephew's songs, accompanied by wild native airs on his accordion.

I remember that morning as if it were yesterday. The bottom was at about eleven fathoms, rougher than any part of the lagoon that we had seen. Here and there pinnacles of coral rose to within a few yards of the surface; in the shadowy depths below, the bottom was seamed with crannies and pitted with the mouths of caves. The look of the place, in fact, was by no means reassuring, but the men sent out to survey the bottom reported that the lagoon there was fairly paved with shell.

It had become my habit to take a water glass in the canoe, for by now I was expert at opening the shell, and I found it interesting, in leisure moments, to watch my companion at his work. The depth was too great to see clearly, but I watched Marama plunge feet-first into the shadows, and a moment later, a second string of bubbles told me that Maruia's nephew had followed him down. Vaguely in the depths I could see Marama moving about, a dim moving shadow when his body passed above a patch of sand. Then, before half a minute had passed, the canoe lurched suddenly and sharply — the native boy was pulling himself up the line in desperate haste.

His head broke water. With a heave and a spring that nearly capsized us, he threw himself into the canoe.

"Ah, the great tonu — he nearly had me!" he panted, trembling with excitement. "Aué! Teura! Where is he?"

I snatched up the water glass, and side by side, with our heads close together, we gazed down into the blue water. Hearing the boy's words, Maruia had seized her own glass. Next moment a sudden sharp wail came from her lips. Then I saw the figure of her nephew, mounting his line with great heaves of both hands — and rising deliberately beneath him a monster hideous as a nightmare memory. It was a huge fish, eight or nine feet long and of enormous bulk. Its great spiny head, four feet across and set with a pair of eyes like saucers, terminated in jaws larger than a shark's; its rough body was spotted and brindled in a way that rendered it almost invisible against the coral; its pectoral fins, frilled and spiny as the fins of a sculpin, spread out like wings on either side. It had the look of an incredibly old and gigantic rock-cod — to which family, indeed, I have been told that the tonu belongs.

We watched in terrible suspense, all three of us. Teura was nearing the surface; in another moment he would be safe. The tonu seemed undecided, as if it were following the man out of curiosity rather than pursuing him. I began to breathe more freely. Then when the diver was within twenty feet of us, the fish reared itself suddenly and came rushing up, huge jaws agape.

In a twinkling it was beneath us, so close that the water beneath the canoes swirled with its passage. The next instant the monster flashed downward and the man was gone.

The tonu halted, four or five fathoms down, and lay with gently moving fins. It was then I saw, to my unutterable horror, that Teura's feet and the calves of his legs hung from the creature's twitching jaws.

Another spectator was close at hand. "Aué!" cried old Maruia bitterly, in a choking voice. "Teura is gone! But I shall kill that devil as he has killed my boy!"

She had been baptized — she was a churchgoer and a keeper of the Sabbath day; but now I heard her half chanting a strange invocation, in loud and solemn tones. "She prays to the heathen gods," muttered Marama in an awed whisper, "to Taiao, and to Ruahatu, the old shark-god of her people!"

I glanced up. The woman was standing in the stern of her canoe. She wore her usual diving-dress, a loose gown of cotton over a pareu worn as the men wore theirs. The goggles were on her eyes and she had taken up a heavy fish-spear from its place on the outrigger-poles of the canoe. It was a formidable weapon, a haft of tough black wood tipped with a yard of steel: a tapering lance sharpened to a needle-point. I turned my head to look into the water glass. The great fish lay beneath us, a monstrous vision in the blue twilight below; but now the man's legs had disappeared.

Maruia's canoe came alongside. I heard the outrigger knock softly against our own. Then both canoes rocked violently, and we started at the sound of a heavy plunging splash.

Without a word to us or an instant's hesitation, Maruia had leaped overboard. One hand held a leaden diving-weight and the other gripped the spear, point downward. The fish scarcely moved at the turmoil in the water; the hideous lord of the lagoon was making his meal. Our hearts beat fast as we watched what followed, gazing through our little pane of glass. Swift and straight, the woman went down head-first till she was within two yards of the tonu's back. She let go the weight, which plunged down out of sight among the shadows; she drew herself together and struck — struck squarely where the head joined the misshapen body, a foot behind the monstrous goggle eyes. I saw the steel strike deep — saw Maruia raise herself upright in the water to drive the spear home with both hands on the shaft. The fish started; its jaws gaped wide — the sprawled and mangled body of Teura eddied down toward the coral forty feet below. The wounded monster turned on his side, the shaft of the spear protruding from his spiny back, and swam feebly and aimlessly to the surface, where the divers, now gathering from all sides, put a quick end to his struggles.

Then I heard the eerie diver's whistle close beside our canoe and the voice of Maruia calling to us. "I am going home," she said. "Lend me a hand to put Teura in the canoe." She had been nearly four minutes under water and had brought up with her the body of her boy.

The natives did no more diving that day. Anchors came up, gear was stowed away, and one after another the canoes fell in behind old Maruia, while the wailing of the *tangi*, the native mourning for the dead, floated across the lagoon. I reached for our own anchor-line, but Marama stopped me with a gesture.

"Wait," he said seriously, "we will go back soon, but first there is something I must tell you."

"Let us go to the Tara," I answered, "and tell Seroni what has happened. This place makes me shudder. I have no more heart for diving to-day."

The native boy looked at me solemnly.

"Like you, I am afraid," he confessed, "but I have seen what moves me more strongly than fear. And I know that our fears are baseless, for my grandfather, who was the most skilled fisherman of Raiatea, has told me many times that where one tonu lives, another is never to be found close by.

"Watch well," he went on, "and move the basket

if there is danger, for I am going down once more. In the cave where I first saw the tonu, are two *parau tahito* — the old oysters of which the divers speak. They are covered with barnacles, very old and huge, and perhaps they hold pearls — great pearls that will make rich men of you and me. But that cave is an evil place! Teura went down with his back to me, and I saw him reach the bottom close to the entrance of the cavern, which he did not see. Then I looked in, and my heart beat fast as I saw that pair of old oysters, just inside. I looked more closely, and there in the shadows were the eyes of the tonu watching me, and his great jaws opening as he made ready to rush out. For a moment my limbs were paralyzed! The rest you saw."

I was becoming infected with my companion's excitement. Ever since we had begun to dive I had heard stories of famous pearls, taken throughout the group in years gone by, and the pearls which fetched the greatest sums and made immortal the names of their finders had always come from these huge, old, and sickly-looking oysters, growing apart from the rest.

Marama had picked up his goggles and was making ready to go over the side, when a saying of my uncle's flashed across my mind. "Never let one of your men do a job you're afraid to do yourself!" Then all at once I knew that I should have no peace unless I acted quickly.

"Stop," I said — a little shakily, at the prospect of the task before me. "You have been down once. Now it is my turn!"

All my life I have found that the more one fears a thing, the quicker it should be done. Without heeding Marama's protests, I snapped on my glasses, tucked up my waistcloth, and went overboard. Next moment I seized the lead-line and signaled Marama to let go.

Never, before or since, have I been more afraid than on that day, as the weight took me plunging down into a bluish gloom. The bottom, as I have said, was at about eleven fathoms, — close to seventy feet, — and since the coral was of the dark-purple kind, the light was very dim. When my weight struck the coral my heart was beating so that I nearly choked; I lost my bearings and wasted half a minute before I found the entrance of the tonu's cave. Suddenly, five yards ahead of me, I perceived the dark mouth of the cavern, like a low wide doorway, fringed with pink coral and gently waving weeds. As I stared into the darkness which seemed to fill a vast chamber, I felt a prickling at the roots of my hair — what if the tonu had a mate!

Then, dimly in the gloom, I made out the forms of the two great oysters, their barnacled and crusted shells agape. I moved forward to wrench them from the rock. With one in each hand I swam toward the basket, glancing back fearfully as I went. There was no shout of triumph when I reached the surface — I flung myself into the canoe and lay there while Marama pulled up the basket.

"You got them?" he inquired eagerly, without turning his head in my direction.

"They are in the basket," I said, "but if I had not found them, I would not have gone down again!"

"My stomach was cold at the thought of it. Come — let us open the shell and leave this evil place. I can scarce wait to see what is inside!"

"You take one," I suggested, "and I will open the other."

"Yes!" he answered, with a boy's eagerness to prolong the moment of suspense, "I will open mine first, and when we have seen what it contains, you can look into the other one."

He inserted his knife close to the hinge, severed the muscle connecting the shells, and laid the great oyster open on the bottom of the canoe. His fingers, skilled with long practice, went under the fringing mantle where nearly all pearls are found, searching rapidly and in vain. He felt more carefully — uttered an exclamation of disgust.

"There is nothing," he said mournfully, "not so much as a blister pearl!"

I took my knife and opened the oyster he had handed me. It was very old and diseased; the shells seemed half rotten, pierced with the holes of borers, and the flesh of the creature inside had a sickly, greenish look. My forefinger went under the mantle — felt something hard and smooth, which moved loosely at the touch. Next moment I laid in Marama's hand a magnificent pearl, the size of a marble, round, flawless, and glimmering with the sheen of perfect orient.

We gazed at it, awed by our good fortune. A man

might spend years among the atolls without laying
eyes on a pearl one half so beautiful! My fingers had
gone back to the oyster to complete the habitual
inspection when Marama found his voice.

"With such a pearl," he said softly, "a man could
buy a schooner like the Tara, or an entire island for
himself! Not one of the divers has ever seen its
match, nor — "

I interrupted him with a frenzied shout, as I laid
in the palm of his hand, beside the first pearl, a second one — its twin in size, in color, in lustre, and
perfection of form.

"Marama," I said when we had grown a little
calmer, "we must say nothing of this to anyone
except Seroni. I know little of pearls, but the value
of this matched pair is too great to be made known!
The sight of them would tempt a man to things he
might regret."

Our mood of exultation was quenched by the
wailing of mourners as we passed the islet, and the
sight of my uncle's sober face when he met us at the
Tara's rail. "I'm glad you came in," he said.
"This has been a bad day and I'm feeling anxious
and depressed. Teura — poor devil; he was one of
the best of the lot; I've known him since he was a
lad at school. This business won't stop the diving,
of course, — it's all part of the day's work to them,
— but it's a pity that such a tragedy has come to
spoil our season at Iriatai. I've been jumpy as an
old woman since the canoes came in — a silly idea
that you might have gone on diving and that there

might have been another of those damned tonus about!"

"We want to have a talk with you, Uncle Harry," I said. "Can we go down to your stateroom — all three of us?"

I followed my uncle and Marama into the stateroom and closed the door behind me. Then I unrolled the tuck of my pareu, opened a knotted handkerchief and laid on the table the twin pearls of the tonu's cave. My uncle's dark brilliant eyes opened wide, his eyebrows went up, and he whistled a soft and long-drawn note. Without a word he took up first one pearl and then the other, turning them in his fingers and letting the light play over their gleaming and flawless surfaces.

"By Jove!" he exclaimed at last, "you take my breath away! I reckon this is the most beautiful matched pair that ever came out of the Paumotus — by long, long odds! In Paris, on the Rue de la Paix, the jewelers would fight one another for a chance to bid on them! You can't set a price on a pair of pearls like these. One of them by itself would make you independent in a small way; the fact that they're matched probably doubles the value of each." He turned to the native boy. "Eh Marama," he said to him, in his own tongue; "you are a lucky boy! This morning's work will make you the richest man of Raiatea, with a fine house, a cutter, and plantations enough to keep all your relatives in plenty. But say nothing of this, for not all men are good at heart."

"Of course they are yours," he went on in English, "to do with as you wish; but I advise you two to let me handle this matter for you. They must be sold as a pair, and I know a Jew on Tahiti who will give us the top of the market. He is buyer for one of the largest firms in Paris, and in a case like this, something more than money is involved. These pearls will make history, you will see; I haven't a doubt they'll end among the jewels of some European court. Sikorsky knows me and knows that I know the game; it will be a matter of naming our own price, within reason, for the acquisition of such a pair of pearls would be a tremendous feather in his cap. Come, we must christen them, for pearls of real importance are always named. What do you say to calling them the *Marama Twins?* Marama means the moon, and their orient has the pure, pale glimmer of moonlight. What beautiful things! If I were a rich man I'd take them off your hands myself!

"See — we'll put them in cotton-wool in this tobacco-tin, and stow it away in the safe. The less said the better, I fancy, even among ourselves. Such a temptation might prove too much for almost any man! But tell me about Teura — his aunt was too much cut up to talk."

Marama left us to go on deck while I told my uncle the story of the morning's happenings. He shook his head when I told of how the canoes had gone home, and of our resolution to go down after the two old oysters Marama had seen. Then I spoke of my feeling that I must be the one to dive, and how I had gone down to bring up the oysters from the tonu's cave.

"I know what you mean," he remarked, as I concluded, "and you did the right thing; but don't take such chances very often! You'll have to keep on diving for a few days, if only for the sake of public morale, but I wish you'd slack off gradually and give it up altogether in a week or two."

IX

THE CAVE OF THE SHARK GOD

I WENT on deck that night and lay alone in the warm darkness, building castles in Spain. Every lad has dreamed of all that he would do for his parents when he had gone out into the world and made his fortune, and now my dreams seemed to have come true at last. I thought of my mother, and the things I might do to brighten the dullness of her life; of Marion, and how my good fortune would send her to the Eastern school she longed for; of my father, who had dreamed for years of improving and restocking the ranch. The old Santa Brigida where I had been born and where I hoped to end my days — a sudden understanding came to me, a rush of gratitude for my father's determined clinging to our land. I realized as never before how I loved the valley, the brown hills, the lonely stretch of coast. A home to go back to — that was the best thing in life!

Teura was to be buried in the morning, and no man on the islet slept that night. After the native fashion the divers were assembled at Maruia's house, and all night long their wild and melancholy songs floated out across the water. The hymns of the islanders have a power to stir one strangely: the voices of the women wailing in a minor key, the deep, chanting refrain of the men — gradually, under the influence of their music, my thoughts wandered, and I fell asleep.

The natives observe Sunday with a strictness unknown among more civilized Christian races. Saving a few unavoidable tasks like cooking, no work of any kind is done on that day, and the man bold enough to break the rule would make an outcast of himself. If he went fishing, they believe that his fishing would be accursed; if by any chance he caught a fish, its flesh would be poisonous; and in all probability a shark would be sent to overturn his canoe and make an end of the impious Sabbath-breaker. White men are a law unto themselves, of course, but my uncle had warned me long since that it would be a mistake to urge Marama to break the rules of his religion. Our Sundays, therefore, were what Sundays should be — days of rest and change from the occupations of the week.

Marama and I often persuaded the cook to put up a cold lunch for us, and set out in our canoe to explore the distant portions of the lagoon. To amuse ourselves, and for easier traveling on these occasions, we had rigged a sail — a bamboo mast, a big leg-of-mutton sail of unbleached cotton, and a spar of tough light wood. We selected from the Tara's stock of lumber a long two-inch plank, and when we set out for a day's sailing this plank was lashed to the canoe — one end to the outrigger, the middle to the gunwales, and the other projecting up and out, six feet on the starboard beam. We carried a tremendous spread of sail for so small a craft, and the long narrow canoe, with a fresh breeze astern or on the beam, skimmed the lagoon at a speed that delighted our hearts. One of us managed the sheet and steered with an oar from the whaleboat; the other took his place on the plank, changing sides when we tacked, and crawling out on the weather beam when the wind freshened and the canoe lay over — bounding forward to rush through the water with a tearing sound.

On the Sunday after Teura's burial, we took our lunch and set out for an all-day sail, and toward the middle of the afternoon the trade wind fell away and died. We were on the west side of the lagoon, a mile or two north of the village of the copra-makers, built on the site of the ancient Paumotan settlement. It was the first time that we had passed close to the place where the shark had met his death, and as we paddled slowly along the coral cliffs rising almost to the surface, we watched for the opening of the cave.

Finally, through the calm blue water, not more than ten or twelve feet down, we saw the mouth of the cavern where the monster had taken refuge. The palms alongshore almost overhung the lagoon at this place. The fringing reef which fell away in a line of submarine cliffs was only a few yards wide, and beyond it lay the highest land on Iriatai, the path of an ancient hurricane where the breaching seas of centuries ago had piled great blocks and masses of coral to a height of eight or ten yards above the sea. Marama dropped his paddle and took up a pair of water goggles.

"Hold the canoe here a moment," he said; "I am going overboard for a look. There was only one shark and I do not believe that a tonu would live so close to the surface."

Next moment he was over the side and swimming down toward the cave-mouth, into which I saw his body disappear. Presently, with leisurely strokes, he swam into sunlit water and rose to take breath, with a hand on the gunwale of the canoe. "Have patience a little longer," he said with a smile, as he pulled down his goggles for the second time. "I am going down once more."

Again he disappeared, and again I waited idly for his reappearance. A minute passed; a minute and a half; two minutes. I began to be alarmed. Three minutes were gone. I knew that never before had my friend stayed down so long. Four minutes —

I hauled up the canoe in the shallows, snapped on my glasses and plunged down to the entrance of the cavern. As I peered in anxiously, I saw that there was a strange glimmer of light where only darkness should have been. Suddenly the light was blotted out, and Marama emerged from the tunnel and rose with me to the surface of the lagoon. When we had taken breath, his hand went up to interrupt my hasty demand for an explanation.

"Aué!" he exclaimed in an excited voice, "but that is a strange place! The hole in the coral rises as it runs inward, and seeing light ahead I thought that I would swim in a little way. The light grew stronger; all at once my head was out of water and

I was breathing air. When I pushed up my glasses to look about me, I found that I was swimming in the midst of a great pool, arched over with a low ceiling of rock. At the farther end a single ray of sunlight shines through a crack between two wedged-in boulders, and beneath the light I saw a broad ledge, sandy and high above the water. On that ledge, where a hundred might stand together, are things of the old times: a heathen god, spears, stone axes, the whitened heads of men. I am afraid, but I will go back if you desire to see."

A sudden memory flashed into my mind — the scent of wood-smoke; the long, shadowy living room at home; my uncle lying in a rawhide chair with his feet against the stones of the fireplace; the missing brig; the savages of Iriatai; the story of the searching-party — beyond doubt we had stumbled on the cave where the cannibals took refuge on that day so long ago!

"There is nothing to fear in old bones," I said. "Lead the way, if you are not weary, and I will follow close behind."

Marama ducked under like a rolling porpoise, to swim down the face of the cliff with long easy strokes, and I swam after him down the cliff and into the faintly luminous gloom. The light grew stronger as we advanced; twenty yards from the entrance my head came out of water and I breathed the welcome air again. We were swimming in a black pool which half filled a long shadowy cavern, illuminated by a beam of sunlight filtering in through a cranny in the rocks. Stalactites of fantastic shape hung from the low roof, and I saw the broad ledge of which the native boy had spoken. We were in the hidden refuge of the savages, the lurking-place of the terrible carcharodon, the shark which had come so near to making an end of my uncle during our early days on Iriatai!

It was an eerie place. We swam to the far end, and my heart was beating faster than usual when my feet touched bottom and we walked out, side by side, upon the ledge. A glance showed me that the place had been a heathen temple of some sort. Under the hole which admitted light stood a small platform of roughhewn coral blocks, a kind of *marae*, like others to be found throughout the Polynesian islands. On the platform, with his misshapen back to the ray of afternoon sunlight, squatted a hideous little god of stone, leering and monstrous, with hands folded on his belly and with a grinning mouth. A semicircle of crumbling skulls lay about the idol, and leaning against the rocky wall I saw carved war-clubs, beautifully fashioned spears, and axes of polished stone. Marama touched my arm.

"Let us go," he whispered. "This is an ill place, indeed! I have heard the old men's tales of the days when there were still wild people in the Paumotus; without doubt that *tiki* is Ruahatu, to whom you heard old Maruia pray. These heads are the heads of men slain here in sacrifice — their bodies were offered to *Atua Mao*, the shark god. Let us go!'

That night, when I was telling my uncle of the

cavern, Maruia came aboard to show him a pearl that she had found. Her eyes gleamed as he translated to her the story of our adventure, and she nodded her head violently in confirmation of each fresh detail.

"Aye," she remarked at the end; "It was thus in the old days among the Paumotan people. On my island, Matahiva, we had such a place; my father has told me how in his childhood the women took refuge there when the warriors went out to meet the men of Rangiroa, raiding in their great canoes. And that stone god was Ruahatu, the Lord of Sharks. For know that the shark you killed was not a shark, nor would you have killed him had you not been a white man! You smile — but I am speaking true words. For a hundred years, two hundred, since time beyond reckoning, perhaps, he has lived in that cave and fattened on the bodies of men, cast to him by the priests. Yet his own people might swim about him fearlessly, for he knew them, and they were of his clan. One of my own ancestors, after his death, took on the semblance of a shark!"

"You'll have an interesting yarn to tell at home," said my uncle, when the woman was gone. "I've heard of these Paumotan refuge-caves, but I never knew a man who had laid eyes on one. Some Sunday we'll run down for a look. I'd like to get those weapons for my collection in Tahiti."

X

THE CHOLITA COMES TO IRIATAI

In those days Marama and I were accounted among the skilled fishermen of the island, and a few weeks after we explored the shark's cave, we decided to make an expedition after a fish seldom captured in the South Seas — the dolphin, or dorado, which the natives called *mahimahi*. He is a noble fish, swift, predatory, and difficult of approach, a rover of the open sea, where his pursuit requires no small degree of hardihood and skill. And the dolphin's flesh is delicate above all other fish — a feast for island kings before the white man came. Pahuri, the Tara's wrinkled engineer, gave us the idea of dolphin-fishing: we were listening to his yarns one night when he chanced to speak of the mahimahi.

"Aye," he said, as he twisted a bit of tobacco in a pandanus-leaf, "there is one fish that you have never caught! How many men on this island have tasted of the dolphin? Not you — nor you?" We shook our heads.

"When I was a boy in the Cook Islands," he went on reminiscently, "that fish was often in the oven at my father's house. In those days the men had not grown lazy and timid, clinging to the land. For it needs a man to bring the dolphin home: he is not to be found in a few fathoms of water close to shore! The mahimahi is the swiftest of all fish and the most beautiful, with his colors of blue and green, changing like flame. He ranges far out to sea in little bands — three or four males and as many females together. You will know them apart easily, for the male will often weigh a hundred pounds, while his mate is never more than half his size. How can you find the dolphin? Listen and I will tell you — I have forgotten more of fishing-lore than these others will know in all their lives!

"Paddle offshore a mile, two miles, three miles, and wait in the early morning calm, when the birds fly out to feed. When you see the *itatae*, the small, pure white tern, watch carefully! Remember that the brown noddy-tern, which follows the bonito, never circles above the mahimahi. But if you see four or five white birds circling low and fast above the waves, hasten to that place and make ready for the dolphin-fishing. As for bait, flying-fish is good, but I will tell you a secret. Above all other food, the mahimahi loves the lobster! Take with you the white meat from the tails of the lobsters, and when your canoe is close to the birds throw this bait into the water directly under them. Then watch closely and you will see the dolphin dart up from the depths like a living flame! Let your baited hook sink slowly and presently a fish will seize it, but you must handle him gently, for he is very swift and strong. If one is taken, the others will stay about the canoe, and you will catch them all. You are going to try? I would go with you if I had time — it is work from daybreak to darkness!"

That night we made torches of dried coconut-leaves, bound in long bundles, and paddled out to the reef separating the two islands north of camp. There was a new moon, by good luck — the best time of the month for lobsters and other dwellers on the barrier. We wore rope-soled shoes to protect our feet from the sharp spines of sea urchins, and when we had anchored the canoe in shallow water we walked abreast along the outer edge of the reef, brightly illuminated by our torches. When a comber toppled and crashed, sending a foaming rush of water across the coral, we halted and waited till the water cleared in the interval before the next breaker came rolling in. Then we walked slowly, bending to scan each weedy crevice and hole. Sometimes a lobster darted like a flash from his refuge and was gone; sometimes the torchlight reflected from a pair of stalk-eyes betrayed our quarry in time for us to press a foot down on the lobster's back, seize him warily from behind, and toss him into the gaping sack. In an hour we had more than we could use.

The stars were shining and there was only the faintest glimmer of dawn, when we dragged our canoe over the reef and shot out seaward through the breakers. Gradually, as we left Iriatai behind us, the eastern sky paled, grew luminous, flushed a rosy pink. The sea changed from black to gray, and from gray to blue — a new day had begun. Around the vast circle of the horizon, saving in the west, where masses of dark cloud towered to a great height, light scattered trade-wind clouds hung above the line where sea met sky.

"I do not like the look of the weather," remarked Marama, glancing westward; "there is wind in those clouds, and if they draw nearer we must return in haste. But the sea is calm, so let us go about our fishing for an hour or two."

We were perhaps four miles offshore. The palms of Iriatai lay like a low smudge along the horizon to the south of us. Singly and in twos and threes, the birds had left their roosting-places ashore and were flying this way and that over the sea, on the lookout for schools of fish. There were boobies and noddy terns in plenty, and a few of the small snow-white terns on which we kept a special watch. Suddenly, a quarter of a mile from us, a pair of noddies began to circle and dive; other birds came flapping hastily from all directions, and soon hundreds of them were wheeling and plunging through the air.

"Bonito," said my companion, heading the canoe toward the school. "Let us make sure of not returning empty-handed!"

It was an old game to me, but one of which I never wearied. We bent our backs and dug our paddles into the sea. The light canoe flew over the swells at a pace that left a wake of foam. I heard Marama drop his paddle; knew that he had turned to face the stern and taken the long bamboo pole from its place on the outrigger-supports. "*Hoe! Hoe!*" he cried. "Paddle your hardest—the school is turning, and in a moment we shall be among them!"

Now the birds were all about us, and the sea was alive with the small fish on which birds and bonito feed, leaping and flashing by thousands in a frenzy of fear. A bonito leaped with a heavy plunge, close to the canoe — another — another; next moment an acre of sea was churned into foam as they fell upon their prey like wolves. I was in the bow place, and now my efforts were redoubled, for everything depended on keeping the canoe in rapid motion. Marama was seated on the stern thwart, facing the rear. In his right hand he held the butt of the rod, braced against the thwart. As the sun was bright, he had selected a dark lure, — a piece of greenish-black mother-of-pearl, fashioned in the shape of a four-inch minnow, — and it skittered along behind us in an extraordinary lifelike way. Cupping his left hand, Marama leaned over the side and began to throw water over the lure, five yards astern — a custom believed to attract the fish. I heard a shout — a fat bonito came tumbling through the air and thumped into the bottom of the canoe. Next instant the hook was free and over the side again, and the native boy was calling: "Paddle! Paddle! You are letting them draw away from us!" For a quarter of an hour, with aching muscles and a dry throat, I held the canoe on the outskirts of the school. At last the pace became too much for me, and I dropped my paddle as the rearmost birds left us in their wake.

We sank into the bottom of the canoe and lay there panting. Marama was worn out, for bonito-fishing is a strenuous sport. In fifteen minutes, after paddling five hundred yards at racing speed, he had hooked and swung into our canoe nearly a score of fish, averaging seven or eight pounds each! It was still calm, and the dugout rose and fell gently on the swell as we lay there resting. The bank of black clouds was moving imperceptibly toward us, blotting out the horizon with an ominous violet gloom. It was time that we went home and I was about to speak when I saw Marama was pointing eastward.

"The dolphin!" he exclaimed, as my eye caught the glint of half a dozen small white birds circling rapidly above the sea. "Shall we paddle out yonder for a try, or shall we leave the mahimahi for another day?"

"Let us chance it," I suggested. "Pahuri knows, and from what he said there must be dolphin yonder. It may be a long time before we see the white birds circle again!"

We were young and far from prudent. In spite of the approaching squall, we headed the canoe away from land and strained at our paddles anew. When first sighted, the birds were not more than half a mile distant, but they were moving slowly away from us, and twice, before we caught up, the fish must have sounded, for the terns ceased their feeding and flew about uncertainly till they fell to circling again. At last the birds were diving fearlessly about the canoe — beautiful little creatures, smaller than a pigeon, with pointed wings and dark, incurious eyes. Remembering Pahuri's advice, I baited my hook and stood up in the bow to throw out morsels of lobster. Then I swung the line around my head and cast far out in front of the canoe.

"*Te mahimahi!*" cried Marama excitedly; and I saw a great fish, gleaming with the colors of a fire opal, dart up from the depths, seize a morsel of bait, and disappear. At that instant the line tautened with a jerk that cut the skin of my hand: I was fast to my first dolphin.

He seemed strong as a wild horse. Fathom after fathom of line hissed over the gunwale and into the sea, at a speed that brought a shout to Marama's lips. Then the fish turned and shot up to the surface, rushing this way and that — a streaking flame of azure in the sea. As the line shortened, Marama leaned over the side, long-handled gaff in hand. The dolphin was growing weary; still fighting, but at a slowing pace, he passed close to the side of the canoe — and the native boy's arm shot out. The dugout lurched and nearly capsized as he brought the fish alongside, the gaff deep-buried in the gleaming back. A stroke of the club, a dying quiver, and we seized gills and tail to drag the fish aboard, exclaiming in excited admiration at the play of gorgeous color on his sides.

I had forgotten the impending squall, and now, as I glanced back toward Iriatai, I saw that there was no land in sight. Sea and sky were merged in a thick gloom; the air stirred uneasily; the black clouds were almost overhead. Marama was cutting short lengths of fishline to make fast the loose articles in the canoe; the fish-blub, the baler, the gaff. He passed me a bit of line. "Tie one end to the thwart and the other to your paddle," he said, "and remember that if we swamp there will be no cause for fear — there is small chance that the sharks will find us. Three times have I been swamped at sea, and each time we lay in the water till the waves had calmed, and reached the land without mishap. Look well to the outrigger-lashings forward there — a turn of line might make them more secure."

I doubt if any other type of craft as small and light would have weathered what our canoe went through in the half hour that followed. Long before the wind reached us we could hear the moaning sound of it and see an unbroken line of white advancing across the face of the sea. Then, after a sharp preliminary gust, the squall was on us, shrieking and raving out of the west.

A spume of torn salt water, white and stinging like sleet, drove from crest to crest of the seas, mingling with horizontal sheets of rain which blinded us as we fought desperately to hold the plunging canoe bow-on. It was then that I began to realize the wonderful seaworthiness of the Polynesian canoe — light, sharp, and high-sided, balanced by its outrigger of hibiscus wood, buoyant as cork. In riding such a sea there were sudden fierce strains on outrigger and outrigger-poles — strains which would have snapped the tough wood in an instant, save for its strong and flexible cinnet-

lashings. Each time a sea came rearing high above
us the bow tossed up to meet the slope of broken
water — rose up and up, surmounted the wave,
and plunged into the seething trough beyond.

"Bale!" Marama was shouting in a voice that
came to me faintly above the screaming of the
wind. "Bale, or we shall be swamped!"

As I leaned back to take up the baler I saw that
the canoe was a third full of water — mingled
sea water and rain. I set to work in a panic, while
Marama fought to hold us head-on to the seas,
with clenched teeth and a steady eye ahead. Working at top speed to throw the water out, I perceived
with a sinking heart that the task was beyond his
strength; we had done our best, but in another
moment the canoe would fill and swamp. Three
times, with a sweep of the paddle that knotted his
muscles as though cast in bronze, Marama saved us
by a miracle. A white-crested roller seized us with
a fierce caprice, spinning the canoe about. Marama's paddle dug deep to swing our bows to meet
the oncoming sea and then, with a crackling sound
audible above the wind, the haft of hard black
wood snapped clean in two.

Next moment the wave burst over the gunwale,
and we were struggling in the sea.

For a time I felt that the end was near. The
water was warm and I was clinging to the outrigger-
pole, but it seemed impossible to breathe. I think
I should have suffocated, without my long experience of diving at Iriatai. My eyes were filled with

Next moment the wave burst over the gunwale, and we were struggling in the sea.

water, and each time I strove to get a breath, the sea broke over me to fill my nose and mouth. Little by little I learned to watch my chance, to fill my lungs hastily at moments when I could get a gulp of air.

Marama worked his way along the gunwale of the swamped canoe and took hold beside me, on the forward outrigger pole. The buoyant wood supported our bodies in the water, and our weight at the forward end held the long hull bow-on. The clouds were breaking to the west; the squall was passing suddenly as it had come. The ocean was calming rapidly, steep breaking seas giving place to a long swell, though for the time being there could be no thought of baling the canoe. Before long we were able to speak of our predicament, and I remember that neither of us mentioned sharks, the subject uppermost in both our minds. It is curious that the white man, like his savage cousins, brown or black, is still the prey of an ancient instinct of the race: Never speak of the evil thing you dread!

If the sharks had found us that day, our end would have been a sudden and a ghastly one.

Toward noon the sun shone out through the last of the storm clouds and the sea had gone down so much that Marama made ready for an attempt to get the water out of our canoe. "You have seen it done at Faatemu," he said; "I will watch the waves carefully till our chance comes — and then you must do your best!"

We swam aft and took our places on either side of the stern, holding the canoe head-on while two or three long swells rolled by. Then, at the beginning of a lull, the native boy gave the signal, and we put all our weight on the stern, sinking it deep. "Now!" cried Marama, and we dove down, pushing it still deeper and thrusting forward as our hands let go their hold. The canoe shot into the air, leaping forward as the light wood bounded to the surface; the hull smacked down on the sea, and a rush of water tumbled forward and poured in a cascade over the bows. Piloted by Marama's skilled hands, she took the next swell without shipping a cupful, her gunwale four or five inches clear of the sea.

"Hold on with one hand and bale with the other," ordered my companion, "and I will swim forward to keep her head-on till she is dry."

There were still a good fifty gallons of water and my task was a weary one, but at last she floated high and one after the other we clambered in gingerly over the stern. Without a word Marama stood up, balancing himself with one bare foot on either gunwale as he gazed out intently to the west.

"There is no land in sight," he said.

I felt no great concern at his words, for I believed the squall could not have carried us many miles offshore and though we had only one paddle between us, a few hours would bring us within sight of the palms of Iriatai. I learned afterward that we were in the clutch of one of the uncharted currents of the Paumotus — a current which swept around the north end of Iriatai and was carrying us farther and farther into the vast stretch of ocean between the coral islands and the South American coast.

Toward three o'clock, while I paddled and Marama scanned the empty line of the horizon from his perch in the bows, he gave a sudden shout. "*E pahi!* — a ship!" he cried, and presently I made her out, a two-masted schooner, hull down in the north. Could it be the Tara, come out in search of us? But no — this was not the first time we had spent a day away from camp; by evening my uncle would begin to feel anxiety, but for the present he would think we had been caught in the squall and forced to land — a stove-in canoe, perhaps, and a weary journey on foot through thorny bush and over sharp and broken rocks.

A light steady breeze ruffled the sea that afternoon, and anxious minutes passed before we made certain that the schooner was heading south. When she was still miles away I saw that she was not the Tara. She carried a pair of lofty topsails, a rare sight in these seas; and unlike the schooners in the island trade, the stranger's mainsail sported a gaff, cocked at a jaunty yachting angle. As she came closer, her towering canvas drawing every ounce of power from the air, she made a picture to delight more critical eyes than mine. The Tara had a sturdy beauty of her own, but she was a "baldheaded" schooner, without topmasts, and she would have had the look of a barge beside the tall, graceful vessel approaching us, skimming the sea like a cup-defender under her press of sail.

Presently she was within hailing-distance and we saw her native crew along the rail. The brown men began to shout questions at us, after the fashion of their race: Who were we — whence did we come — where were we going? Then I heard a command, in a roaring voice that made the sailors spring to their posts. The schooner shot into the wind with a crisp shiver of canvas, bobbing and ducking into the head sea as she moved forward and lost way close alongside. Lines were passed down, strong hands came out to help us; the next moment our canoe lay on deck and we were standing beside it, surrounded by good-natured islanders who were chattering, gesticulating, grinning with flashes of their white teeth.

Again the roaring voice boomed out from astern: "Back the fore-staysail! Eh, Tua! Send the Kanaka forward and bring the white boy aft to me!"

Tua, the mate, a tall native with a handsome determined face, touched my arm. Walking aft while the schooner filled away again, I had my first look at the helmsman, a white man of herculean build. He wore a suit of drill, freshly starched and ironed, snowy yachting-shoes, and a Panama of the finest weave. The lower part of his face was concealed by heavy moustaches and a thick blond beard, but the skin above his cheek-bones was smooth as a woman's. His eyes were of a blue I have never seen before nor since: dark and sparkling when his humor was good — in anger, glittering with the cold glare of ice. In some subtle way the eyes reflected the man's whole personality, at once virile, magnetic, daring, unscrupulous, and cruel. But I was young and his cordial manner disarmed me; for the time, my eyes were not open to the evil in our rescuer. He smiled and stretched out a hand to me — an enormous hand with fingers like so many bananas.

"Well, young man," he said, his deep voice and the order of his words carrying a foreign hint, "from where are you come? In that direction, South America is the nearest land!"

I had asked for water as I stepped aboard, and now a black man with a great shock of hair came aft to hand me a pitcher and a glass. The captain watched me, smiling behind his beard as I drank the water to the last drop. Finally I set down the glass.

"Excuse me, sir," I said, "I was very thirsty! It was lucky for us that you happened to pick us up. We went fishing this morning and our canoe was swamped in a squall. Afterward, when the clouds passed, the land was out of sight, and we've been paddling ever since." He glanced down at a chart unrolled before him on the cockpit floor.

"From Iriatai you are come, then," he remarked. "That is strange, for the island is marked as uninhabited. Well, it is not far out of my course — I am bound for Mangareva to load shell."

His courteous manner and lack of curiosity made me feel that it would be boorish to be reticent. I had no suspicion that he was feeling me out for information. And my uncle had nothing to conceal.

"My name is Selden," I told him, "and I have been on the island several mouths. My uncle, Henry Selden, has leased Iriatai from the Government and planted coconuts. Last year he discovered a patch of shell in the lagoon, and the French have granted him a season's diving-rights."

I was going to say more, but a sudden sound interrupted my words. The ship's bell rang out two sharp and measured beats, paused, and sounded twice again. It was six o'clock. The watch was changing, and at a word from the captain the tall mate came aft to take the wheel.

"Keep a man aloft," the skipper said. "It grows dark, but within half an hour you will raise the land." He turned to me. "Come below," he suggested, "you will be hungry after your day at sea. When we have dined, I shall be interested to hear more of your island."

He followed me down to the saloon, where the table was set with shining glass and porcelain. A young woman rose as we appeared, a slender, graceful girl, with sullen eyes and a great bruise disfiguring one pale brown cheek. She wore a loose gown of scarlet silk; crescents of gold were in her ears; and her dark hair, dressed in a single braid thick as a man's arm, hung to her knees. I learned afterward that she was a half-caste from the Carolines. The captain spoke to her and glanced at me.

"Madame Schmidt," he said in introduction; and as I took her hand, I realized suddenly how I must have appeared. It was months since scissors had touched my hair, which stood on my head like a Fijian's, tangled and bleached by the sun. My skin was tanned to a sort of saddle-color, and I was naked save for the torn and faded pareu about my waist. The captain seemed to divine my thought.

"Eh, Raita!" he ordered, "get out for our guest some clean clothes. He will feel more at ease."

I slipped into a stateroom to put on the garments the woman laid out for me: an enormous pair of trousers I rolled up at the bottom, and a coat in which Marama and I could have buttoned ourselves with room to spare. The meal was served by the captain's body servant, the black, shock-headed savage I had seen on deck. He was an evil-looking creature, like some fierce ape masquerading in a sailor's clothes. Several times during the meal Schmidt gave him orders in an outlandish jargon I had never heard, and once, when the captain told him to fetch wine, he asked his master a question in a shrill chatter, grimacing with his eyebrows like a monkey. The woman ate sullenly, without once raising her eyes; when she had finished, she rose and left us without a word.

It was still daylight outside, but the swinging lamp above the table was lit, and under its light I had an opportunity to study the features of my host. I began to change my first opinion of him, for the scrutiny was not reassuring: the more I looked, the more he puzzled me and the less I trusted him. When the black man set cups of coffee before us

Schmidt began to question me. How long had we been on Iriatai? How many divers were at work? Was there plenty of shell? Was its quality good? Had we been lucky with pearls? But by now I was on my guard, and returned evasive answers, feigning the stupidity of weariness — a deception which did not require much acting on my part. A long-drawn shout from above brought us suddenly to our feet.

"Land ho!"

When I came on deck the western sky was glowing with a fiery sunset, and under the crimson clouds I could make out the long dark line of Iriatai. Puzzled and vaguely uneasy in my mind, I was leaning on the rail when my eye fell on a handsome dinghey, slung on davits close to where I stood. Her stern was toward me, and there, neatly lettered on the bright varnished wood, I saw the word, "Cholita." So Schmidt's vessel was called Cholita — a pretty name for a pretty schooner — and then I remembered with a sudden start. My thoughts flashed back to the morning when I had paddled out to breakfast with my uncle in Faatemu Bay — to his account of Thursday Island Schmidt. My uncle's words came back to me: "His schooner's as pretty as her reputation is black, and the way he handled her was a treat to watch."

So this was the Cholita, and I was the guest of the famous Thursday Island Schmidt!

I felt a touch on my shoulder. Marama was beside me, a serious expression on his face. "Listen!"

he said in a hurried whisper; "I must go forward
before the captain returns. If we approach the
land to-night, let us slip overboard and swim ashore.
Seroni must be warned, for I think that there is
evil afoot. Do you remember Rairi, the Tara's
cook who tried to kill old Pahuri that night on our
passage south? He is aboard — I have seen him,
though his face was turned away from me. He has
been ordered to keep out of your sight. This
schooner was bound for Iriatai before she picked
us up. The mate, who is a good man and beginning to fear for himself, has told me as much."

The captain was approaching with a noiseless
step; when I glanced up he was not four yards off.
He halted and looked at Marama in angry astonishment. "Get forward," he bellowed, in a voice
that made the sailors turn their heads, "*verdammt*
Kanaka cheek!" He turned to me, the former
suavity gone from his manner. "And you," he
ordered — "go below!"

I obeyed him, choking with anger and a sense of
impotence. The half-caste girl was sitting on the
lounge, she had been sewing, but now her hands
were clenched and her work lay where it had dropped
to the floor. There was a look of apprehension in
her eyes. When she saw that I was alone she beck-
oned me with a swift gesture.

"Come here, boy — me want talk with you,"
she whispered in quaint broken English. "Me hear
Schmidt say 'Go below' — he too much bad man!
Guk! Me hate him! — Suppose we go near land

tonight, me jump overboard, swim ashore. You come too — we go hide in bush."

Her fierce eyes blazed as she pointed to the bruise on her cheek.

"Schmidt do that yesterday," she went on. "Me like kill him, but too much 'fraid! Before, me think him good man. My father white man — same you. Me, my mother, live Ponape, Caroline Island. One day Cholita come — everybody think Schmidt good man — spend plenty money — have good time. Every day he come my house. By and by he say: 'To-morrow I go 'way; you my friend — give me orange, pig, drinking-coconut. To-night you bring old woman aboard — we have big *kaikai.*' My mother think he good man — we go. Schmidt bring us aboard schooner — we eat, play accordion, have good time. Pretty soon hear noise on deck. My mother stand up. 'What that?' she say. Then Kwala hold old woman — Schmidt throw me in stateroom — lock door. Outside reef he throw my mother in canoe — tell her go ashore. Porthole open — me hear old woman crying — Guk! Schmidt never let me go ashore. In Tahiti — Noumea — me 'fraid — he say suppose me swim ashore, send police fetch."

Her quick ear caught the sound of a footstep on deck and she signaled me hurriedly to move away. Next moment Schmidt came down the companion-way, glancing at the woman sharply. Without a word he motioned me into the stateroom, slammed the door behind me, and turned the key.

I heard Raita's voice raised in protest, and the captain's gruff reply. Then the companionway creaked under his weight as he went on deck again.

Until now I had viewed the Cholita and her master in an adventurous light; but as I lay there in the dark behind a locked door I began to feel anxious and a little afraid. Little by little, as realization grows at such a time, I put together the scattered recollections in my mind: what my uncle had said of Schmidt; the half-caste girl's story; the presence aboard the Cholita of Rairi, our former cook; the old letter, telling of the gold-lipped shell in Iriatai lagoon; Rairi's stealthy visit to the Tara after his discharge; Schmidt's treatment of me; Marama's words, and the brutal stopping of our conversation. There was small room for doubt — each detail fitted perfectly into the story taking form in my mind.

While the schooner lay alongside the Papeete wharf (I thought), discharging the load of shell of which my uncle had spoken, Rairi must have made the acquaintance of Schmidt. Our one-time cook had looked through the papers snatched up in hope of doing my uncle an injury, and had come upon Turia's letter, written to her son. It was a chance in a thousand, but how was Rairi to make use of it? Then, meeting Schmidt and knowing something of his character from gossip along the waterfront, the vengeful Paumotan must have seen his opportunity. A few cautious questions to feel out his man, increasing confidence, the final disclosure of Turia's old letter — and the compact made. It would be a daring bit of robbery in these modern days; I wondered how Schmidt could hope to keep out of trouble in the long run. He might scuttle the Tara, of course, and leave us marooned on Iriatai, but our whereabouts was known to many people, and before many months had passed some-one was bound to set out with a schooner to see what had become of us. But he was a resourceful scoundrel, from all I had heard; he must have weighed his chances before embarking on such a piece of barefaced piracy. And robbery was the Cholita's errand. I knew it now as surely as if Schmidt had disclosed his plans to me.

As I lay there in the berth, tired and frightened, I began to blame myself for not having played a more cunning game. Now that my chance had gone, I saw that I might have played the part of a talkative and unsuspecting lad, answered Schmidt's questions freely, and perhaps have kept my liberty until we drew near the land. Then I might have gone overboard in the darkness, made my way to my uncle and given him warning of the Cholita's approach. Now it was too late. They would take the Tara by surprise. There might be bloodshed. A terrible thought flashed into my mind — Uncle Harry stretched out on his schooner's deck —

I sat up in the berth, clenching my hands. I had no dearer friend in the world. But at last excitement and weariness overcame my anxious thoughts, and I fell into a dreamless sleep.

When I awoke the morning sun was shining through my porthole, and looking out, I saw that we lay close to the beach, just inside the pass of Iriatai. A noise of thumping and scrubbing overhead told me that the decks were being washed down. We were at anchor, I knew, for the schooner lay motionless, though the current at this place was strong. An hour passed and as I craned my neck out the port I saw the Cholita's dinghey approaching us from the north. The handsome little boat drew near and I saw Rairi in the stern, a Winchester across his knees and a bandolier of cartridges over one shoulder. Schmidt's shockheaded black was at the oars and at his feet a man lay in the bottom of the dinghey — an elderly native, bound hand and foot, his gray head matted with blood and unsheltered from the sun. It was Pahuri — I knew with a sudden breathlessness that they had taken the Tara and that Rairi was enjoying a savage's revenge.

The dinghey passed out of my sight around the schooner's stern. I heard the thump of a body flung down roughly on the after deck, Rairi's voice raised in a sharp command, and the creak of the davit-blocks as the boat was hoisted to the rail. Then, for a long time, all was quiet. Rairi had gone below for a rest and a nap, leaving the black on guard, for most of the crew were new men whom neither Rairi nor Schmidt would trust too far. Finally the silence was broken by a weak voice — old Pahuri begging monotonously for water. Heavy steps came aft over my head and I heard the mate order the black man to give water to his prisoner. But the savage chattered a refusal in his own uncouth tongue; he had a rifle and he was under orders from Rairi, so Tua strode forward angrily, muttering to himself. Then suddenly I heard a rapid whispering at the keyhole of my door. It was Raita.

"Eh, boy!" she said, "listen — you asleep?"

"No," I whispered back.

"Last night," she went on, "Schmidt take your schooner — Rairi bring back old man he no like. I sorry that man — head hurt — too much blood. Rairi leave him in sun — no give water. Schmidt stop aboard your schooner — suppose wind come up, Cholita go there. Native boy, your friend, swim ashore last night. Me think go too, then think no — me stop aboard, maybe help you. Ah — me hear Rairi — me go!"

I heard her move away, quickly and softly, from the door. Her words added little to my anxiety, for Pahuri's presence told me that Schmidt had captured the Tara, but the thought of my uncle tortured me: Where was he — captured, wounded, perhaps dead? I glanced out the porthole. The palms were swaying to the first of the trade wind, heralded by long blue streaks outside the pass. Presently there were sounds of activity on deck; shouting and creaking of blocks as they hoisted the foresail, the deep-voiced chant of the sailors at the windlass. Then, heeling a little to the freshening breeze, the Cholita filled away on the port tack, turned to leeward as she gathered way, and slacked off for the long run across the lagoon.

When we drew near the islet, toward midday, I saw that the Tara's anchorage had been changed: she was lying fully a quarter of a mile off shore. Eight bells struck as we rounded into the wind beside her; I heard the anchor plunge overboard and the prolonged rattle of the chain. Then the bellowing voice of Schmidt hailed us, shouting orders and instructions. A moment later the key turned in the lock of my door and Rairi entered to grasp me by the arm.

"Come," he said roughly, "Schmidt want you aboard Tara!"

He half dragged me up the companionway and across the deck, where I had a glimpse of our engineer lying bound in the sun, his gray hair clotted with blood. Rairi motioned me into the dinghey alongside, sprang in after me and signed to the oarsman to pull us across to the Tara. Schmidt was standing by the rail.

"Where's the Kanaka boy?" he asked.

"Swim ashore last night; maybe shark take him — no matter."

"Let him go — no harm can he do us. Wait for me."

I clambered over the rail in obedience to Schmidt's gesture, and he followed me below. My uncle's stateroom was open and in great disorder. We halted opposite the door of my own cabin. The German drew from his belt a heavy Colt's revolver, cocked it, unlocked the door quickly, and pushed me inside. As I stood there, dazzled by the bright light of the porthole, I heard the key turn behind me, and then my uncle's quizzical voice.

"Well, old fellow," he remarked, "it's good to see you safe and sound. We seem a bit down on our luck, eh?"

He was lying in my berth, quietly puffing one of his long, thin cigars.

XI

PIRACY

FOR a moment I was overcome by astonishment
and relief; my mouth half opened and tears came
into my eyes. My uncle stretched out his hand.

"Cheer up!" he said, smiling at my long face.
"We're not beaten yet! Before I tell you my side
of the yarn, let's hear how our friend Thursday
Island happened to pick you up."

Speaking in a low voice, I told him of our fishing,
of the squall, how the canoe was swamped, how we
had baled her, and how Schmidt had picked us up.
His only comment was a soft whistle when I spoke
of how I had nearly drowned before the sea went
down. Then I told him of the Cholita: her captain,
the half-caste girl, Rairi, and the story I had pieced
together. As I finished, Uncle Harry nodded his
head.

"That's it," he remarked — "not a doubt! That
scoundrel Rairi — I wish I'd handed him over to
the authorities as I was tempted to do! I wish also
that I hadn't built my stateroom doors so well;
they're solid oak, an inch and a half thick, with
hinges and locks to match! And Schmidt took care
to clear away everything movable: even the water-
bottle's gone! But I must tell you about last night.

"You know the family next door to Maruia's
house — their baby died yesterday, and when dinner

was over I gave the men permission to go ashore for the singing. It was careless, of course, but we've never stood an anchor watch since we've been here. Pahuri stopped aboard — he was asleep up forward — and I was in a pareu, working on my ledger. I keep the books in the safe, you know, and the door of the safe, like the stateroom door, was open. At about eleven o'clock I heard a boat bump softly against the Tara's side, but Fatu was due to bring the men aboard and I paid no attention to the sound. I glanced up from my work a moment later, and there was Mr. Thursday Island Schmidt in the doorway, with a big revolver cocked and aimed at my chest. He requested me, very politely, to hold up my hands and keep them there, and as my own gun was in a drawer behind me, I could see no way of refusing him!

"The only men with Schmidt, I believe, were Rairi and some sort of outlandish nigger. All I saw of the black man was a glimpse of his fuzzy head outside the door, but Schmidt still keeping me covered, ordered Rairi in to go through the contents of the safe. He wanted to get me out of the way, but he saw that the safe was open and he was too wise to turn his back on his partner, even for a moment. He's a cheeky devil, Rairi: he gave me a sour grin that must have done him good. First he pulled out the little drawer where I keep my loose money for emergencies — about a thousand dollars in gold. He laid it on the table, and as Schmidt glanced down I was tempted to have a go at him. But I

knew his reputation, and I knew that Rairi was
aching for a chance at me. At that moment, when
I was half decided to try to knock Schmidt out, I
was distracted by a glimpse of something that
escaped him altogether. Out of the corner of my
eye I saw Rairi's hand shoot out suddenly behind
his back and come up to his waist, where he seemed
to fumble for an instant with the tuck of his pareu.
I looked more closely — one of the small round
tobacco-tins was missing from the row on the shelf!
Rairi stooped down as though he had just perceived
them, gathered the little boxes in a double handful,
and stepped across the room to lay them on the
table beside the drawer of gold. 'Pearls, perhaps,'
he said.

"Schmidt showed signs of interest at that. He
ordered Rairi to open them, and gave each lot a
glance, one after the other, but he never relaxed his
watch on me. Thursday Island is not a man to
trifle with — he's proved that over and over again!
'A nice lot of pearls, Mr. Selden,' he observed, grinning behind his beard; 'there will be a sensation on
Tahiti when they learn that the gold-lipped shell
has been acclimatized. The Government will owe
you a debt for the discovery.'

"I'd been keeping an eye on the pearls and when
the last tin was opened I saw that the Twins were
missing: by the purest chance, Rairi's thieving hand
had landed on their box. I was on the point of telling Schmidt that the pearls he had seen were not
bad, but that the finest of the lot were in the tuck of

his partner's waistband. I don't know why I did n't speak, — they might have had a row which would have given me my chance — but for some reason I kept my mouth shut. When Rairi had made a bundle of my papers and made sure that there was nothing else of value in the safe, Schmidt told him to clear all the loose stuff out of the stateroom across the way. Then he invited me to make myself at home here until his business was done. He spent some time in assuring himself that the door and lock were strong. 'It may ease your mind,' he said, polite as a dancing-master, 'to know that your nephew is safe; I picked him up yesterday at sea; he'll join you presently.'

"They must have overlooked Pahuri when they first came aboard. As the German left my door I heard a racket up forward: that half-caste, mauling the old man in a way that made me see red. I was fool enough to try to break down the door until Schmidt bellowed out something that stopped the noise."

My uncle held up his hands to show me the knuckles, bruised and clotted with blood.

"The noise must have given the alarm to Fatu," he went on, "for a few minutes afterward he put off with Ivi and Ofai in the boat. The current had swung the Tara around so that I could see what followed out of the porthole. Schmidt heard them launching the boat and called his men. He had a powerful electric torch and when he flashed it toward the land I saw my boys taking their places at the oars, Fatu in the stern, and ten or a dozen divers on the beach. Schmidt growled out an order to his partner and I heard Rairi's voice raised to warn the boat away. But our men paid no attention; the light showed them making for the Tara at top speed.

"'Let them have it, then!' bawled Thursday Island. I heard two rifles crack, the snap and click of the levers, and two more quick shots. Ivi dropped his oar and sank down on the grating with a hand to his shoulder. Fatu sprang to his feet, snatched up the oar, and took the wounded man's place, to pull straight for the schooner. Rairi and the nigger would have slaughtered them like sheep, but they held their fire when I shouted through the porthole, telling my men to go back; that a strange schooner was in the lagoon, that her skipper had made me prisoner, and that they had best leave the affair in my hands. There isn't a gun of any sort ashore and I don't want to be rescued at the cost of half a dozen lives! Well, they obeyed me and went ashore. The sound of the shooting roused the whole camp — things have been humming ever since. Perhaps Fatu has some scheme for setting me free; Schmidt seems to think so at any rate, for he and his men went to work on the windlass, got the anchor off the bottom, and allowed the Tara to drift offshore with the current before they anchored her again. As for the fix we're in, the worst that can happen is that we'll lose our pearls. I doubt if even Schmidt has the audacity to load a hundred tons of shell under the noses of the men ashore — I wonder if he would dare? What sort of crew has he — many men he can trust for this sort of villainy?"

I said that I believed most of Schmidt's men were newly shipped, that aside from Rairi and the black they seemed an average lot of natives, not particularly bad. From Marama's words and what I had seen of the man himself, I judged that Tua, the mate, was a first-class fellow, beginning to feel qualms about the company in which he found himself.

"Tua," remarked Uncle Harry, musingly, "Tua — that's not a common name! Did he ship in Papeete? He is n't by any chance a youngish chap, rather light brown and more than six feet tall? That's the man? By Jove! I'd like fifteen minutes alone with him — he's Maruia's foster son!"

A sound of voices put an end to our talk. Schmidt and the black man had come across in the dinghey and were making her fast alongside. Raita was with them, for I heard the captain order her roughly to climb aboard. There was a step on the deck overhead; a sound made me look up and I saw that a basket of food had been lowered to our porthole. Schmidt hailed us.

"I am sorry, Mr. Selden," he said, "that your lunch comes late. For me, these are busy days!" He spoke with a kind of cool politeness he had not troubled to affect toward me. I never heard any man speak rudely to my uncle; even now, while he lay helpless to resent an injury, Schmidt chose to address him courteously. Water was to be had

at the tap, and we ate with good appetites while
Schmidt conversed with my uncle through the
stateroom door. He had come below for a yarn,
he said, and he seemed in a communicative mood.

"My friend Rairi," he began abruptly, "does
not love that old man of yours. Last night, when
he tied his hands, he hurt him more than I thought
necessary — I believed that he was taking him
back to the schooner that he might bind up his
wounds. To-day I found that old man delirious in
the sun, and I was forced to speak plainly. Ach!
A savage — I have had more than enough of the
native — It would be good if business did not
deprive me of your company."

"See here, Schmidt," remarked my uncle good-
naturedly, "do you realize that this business of
yours is apt to deprive you of all company except
your own, for a good many years to come? You
have brains, man — use them! So far, you've played
your cards well: we'll grant that you are able to
get away from Iriatai with the pearls. You know
pearls. I'll be frank: they're worth forty or fifty
thousand at least. But think of the future — you
can't do this sort of thing nowadays. Matters
were different twenty years ago. Sooner or later
this affair will be the talk of the Pacific. Think of
the wireless, man — they'll be looking for you in
every port in the world! Don't mistake me, —
I'm not telling you this for your own good, — but
the lawyers have a very unkind name for what
you are doing. Think it over, Schmidt. If you're

wise, you'll return what you've taken and clear out of Iriatai. As a matter of fact I rather admire your nerve. If you'll turn over Rairi to me, I'll let the matter drop at that."

The answer to my uncle's words was a rumbling chuckle; I could fancy the ironical glint in the German's cold blue eyes. "A handsome offer," he said mockingly. "You are more than kind! Since you are good enough to be frank, I will be frank as well. As for thinking, mine was done long ago. I do not fear all the warships and all the wireless in the world! There can be no harm in telling you, for that matter; in estimating my chances of escape, you can amuse yourself for the next day or two.

"This morning I took my glasses and had a look ashore. A nice stack of shell you have made ready for me, under the shed! That I must have. If there is trouble in loading it and any of your men are hurt, they will have themselves to blame. Bloodshed I do not like: it is always foolishness! Without an axe you will not break out of your stateroom. Matches I have left you and you could set fire to the schooner, but that would be for you unpleasant and would only save me trouble in the end. If you should succeed in breaking out, always there will be one of my men to deal with. Kwala, the black, is a Malaita boy — not a man to trifle with. And Rairi I do not trust overmuch myself; he is a primitive, and he bears you an old grudge. I was nervous last night when he brought me in through the pass;

did you know that long ago he lived on this island?
Yes — his mother was one of the savage women
deported by the French. So you see, I put you out
of my mind."

"Well," said my uncle in an amused voice, "suppose you do load the shell and get away from Iriatai. Can't you see that your troubles would only
be beginning then?"

"Ach, Mr. Selden," said Schmidt with reproach-
ful irony, "you do me injustice! Remember, please,
I am a man of resource. There can be no harm in
it: I shall open my heart to you and tell the truth
— what my vulgar Australian friends used to call,
in their picturesque way, the 'straight griffin,' or
the 'dinkum oil.' First of all, much though I regret,
I must scuttle your pretty Tara. When I am ready
to leave and the holes are bored, the key will be
given you through the porthole in time, that you
may swim to land before the schooner goes down.
Your boats I shall tow to sea with me. I hope you
are not foolhardy enough to venture to sea in the
native canoe. Many months will pass before information can be laid against me. One chance I take
— that a schooner might put in here soon after I
leave; but that chance is small. Like your schooner,
the Cholita is of French registry now; on paper,
my mate, Tua, is her captain; I am cleared for the
Paumotus, to pick up copra and shell. What shall
I do? The simple thing, which all my life I have
found the wisest: go straight to Tahiti, sell my
cargo to the highest bidder, and clear once more

for the Paumotus within a week. As for the gold-
lipped shell, there will be a hint of a discovery in a
remote lagoon; I can see now the wise ones among
the traders hastening to a place five hundred miles
from Iriatai! My men may talk, but two things
will close their mouths, I think — love of money
and fear of me. Clear of Tahiti, my beard and
my schooner's topmasts will come off; she will have
a new name and a new set of papers. At filling them
out, I am clever — you would be surprised! Then,
one fine day, long before they have come to look
for you on Iriatai, a strange schooner will put into
a far-away port, South America, perhaps, or among
the Dutch East Indies — Ach — who knows? There
is a Chinaman in Gillolo who would gladly take
the schooner off my hands. It is a sad thing to grow
old, my friend; I am tired of the Pacific and of this
wandering life. Much is forgotten in twenty years;
it is my dream to settle quietly in the German
village where I was born—But you must excuse me
— I hear my good Rairi calling!"

I heard Rairi's voice and the sound of Schmidt's
footsteps as he climbed on deck. Then all was silent
for an hour or more, while my uncle and I spoke
in low tones of our predicament. Suddenly there
was a whispering at our door — the voice of Raita,
the half-caste girl.

"Eh, boy," she said rapidly, "you hear me? No
talk loud — Kwala, that black man, on deck!
Schmidt, Rairi, they go aboard Cholita. You got
kaikai — got water? Good — me 'fraid you hungry.

Listen: Raita tell you what they do. Schmidt go Cholita tell that mate, Tua, go ashore. Tua tell people on island stop in bush to-morrow; suppose they come on beach, they get shot! When Tua come back, Schmidt, Rairi come aboard this schooner sleep. Keep pearls here. When dark, maybe me swim ashore hide in bush."

"Raita," I called softly, as a sudden idea came to me, "wait by the door for a minute. I want to speak to you when I've talked with my uncle."

I climbed into the upper berth and squeezed my head and shoulders through the porthole. It was as I thought; no man could have passed through such a narrow aperture, but the feat was possible for a slender boy. "Listen, Uncle Harry," I whispered as I climbed down to his side, "you heard what that woman said; now see what you think of the plan I have in mind. Schmidt has sent Tua ashore to warn the people to keep away from the beach while he loads our shell. Tua, you say, is Maruia's foster son, and I feel sure that he and most of the crew are uneasy in their minds. This is my plan: we can see the shore from our porthole, and if, by the time it is dark, Tua has not returned to the Cholita, I will wriggle through the port and swim ashore. It will be easy, I think, to explain the situation to Tua and to our divers. Tua can go off to the Cholita and tell his crew what kind of venture they are engaged in. Once they understand, I'm sure there won't be a hand raised to help Schmidt to-night. Then, in the darkness after the moon

has set, I'll swim off quietly with Fatu, Ofai, and a
few of the divers, climb aboard and take the Tara
by surprise. Once we have Schmidt and his two
followers, there'll be no trouble with the others, I
think. We must decide quickly — let me try!"

For a moment, while I waited in suspense, my
uncle puffed meditatively at his cigar. His eyes were
half closed and he seemed scarcely to have heard
what I had said. Suddenly, with a shrug of his
shoulders, he spoke.

"Very well, Charlie — see what you can do.
But take care of yourself. Remember that I'd
rather lose the Tara and all the shell than have
anything happen to you! It's the devil to have to
sit here helpless while those scoundrels sail away
with our property. I was beginning to believe they
held the winning cards! You've a level head, old
man; this plan of yours has a chance of working
out, I should say. Can you really squeeze through
that porthole? By Jove! I'd give something to
have the laugh on our friend Herr Schmidt!"

Before he had finished I was at the door.
"Raita!" I whispered; and when I heard her answering voice, I told her that I planned to escape through
the porthole and swim ashore. Knowing her hatred
of Schmidt, I confided the fact that we were going
to attack the schooner that night, and begged her
to leave a rope's end hanging over the stern. The
girl was all eager excitement. The blood of a fierce
and vengeful people ran in her veins.

"Guk!" she exclaimed. "Maybe you kill Schmidt,

eh? Me too much happy! Stop aboard now. That other man — tell him when plenty dark me get axe from galley. He watch porthole, eh? Suppose you come aboard — he break door, go help kill Schmidt! Guk! Me like see that!"

"It's lucky you made friends with her," remarked my uncle quizzically, when Raita was gone; "I should dislike to have that young lady for an enemy! Well, if she does n't forget that axe, I'll do my best to entertain her!"

XII

"BOARDERS!"

THE sun went down that night behind banks of crimson clouds, which grew black as twilight gave place to darkness and blotted out the young moon sinking in the west. The evening was calm, but the night promised to be a stormy one. The Tara still lay broadside to the beach and a close watch informed us that Tua had not left the islet. My time had come.

Our chief concern was to make no sound which might give the alarm to the sharp ears of the savage on watch. Pulling together the curtains of the lower berth and muffling the operation in blankets to avoid the slightest noise, we tore a sheet into strips and braided a length of clumsy cord. Then in the upper berth my uncle knotted our rope to one of my ankles, and very gently and cautiously I began to squirm my way out through the porthole. It was a tighter fit than I had supposed; after a twist or two it seemed to me that I could neither move forward nor go back. I was naked save for a pair of swimming trunks, and several square inches of my skin remained on the porthole's sharp brass rim, but at last I was through, hanging by one leg with my head and arms in the water. Knowing that the least splash would bring Kwala instantly to the side, my uncle lowered me little by little into the lagoon, until I lay motionless in the black water and the end of the cord fell into my outstretched hand. I undid the knot, heard Uncle Harry's faintly breathed "Good luck!" and dove without a sound. It was not yet fully dark and I feared that the black man's eyes might discern my head in the reflections of the sunset. Thirty yards nearer the shore I rose to the surface and expelled the breath gently from my lungs. All was quiet aboard the Tara. I had neither been seen nor heard.

I landed under an overhanging thicket of hibiscus, in a little cove where Marama and I kept our canoe hauled up. There were no lights in the doorways that I passed, but when I came to Maruia's house I found the population of the islet assembled there, women and children outside and the divers in the house, surrounding Maruia and Schmidt's mate who sat in earnest conversation on the floor. The light of a lamp shone on the pair and I saw that Tua's face wore an expression of dejection and perplexity. A murmur of astonishment went up as I arrived, and indeed I must have presented a strange appearance — wet, nearly naked, bleeding in a dozen places. Maruia rose and put an arm about me, patting my bare shoulder softly.

"Ah, Tehare," she said, "you have escaped from that wicked man — that is good. And Seroni, your uncle?" I told her how we had been imprisoned in the stateroom, and how I had escaped through the porthole, too small for the broader shoulders of a man. Then I asked for news of Marama.

"He is here," she answered, leading me to her bed, screened off with mats in a corner of the spacious room; "see, he sleeps, and we must not wake him. He followed the western shore on foot, hastening to warn Seroni, but when he came here it was too late. His feet are cut to ribbons by the coral and the sun has given him a fever; I have bandaged his wounds and brewed a tea of herbs. But come — there are other things of which we must speak." She led me back through the crowd and pointed to Tua.

"This man is my foster son," she said, "a good man, but he serves an evil master. He brings us a message from that German that we must go to the far end of the islet while our shell and Seroni's is carried away. Tua is greatly troubled in his mind. He has signed papers and the white man's laws are strict. Furthermore those men are fierce and wary; they are armed with rifles, while we have none. What are we to do?"

I turned to the mate. "Saving Schmidt and the black and Rairi," I asked him, "are the others of the Cholita's crew good men?"

"I know them all," he replied, "and they are like others of their kind, neither good nor bad. But like me, they are in fear of Schmidt and of the white man's prison."

"Listen, then," I went on, "and I will show you how to act the part of honest men. Schmidt is indeed an evil captain and to stand by him means prison in the end. My own ears have heard him say that after he has stolen our pearls and our

shell he plans to sell the schooner and leave you
deserted and friendless in a foreign land. Take
warning, therefore, while there is time. You have
heard of Seroni — Maruia will tell you whether
he or Schmidt is the more to be trusted. Give
heed to my words, then. Schmidt and that dog
Rairi await your coming on the Cholita. Go to
them now and tell them that you have delivered
their message; that the people will obey, being
unarmed and in fear of the rifles. In a little while
those two men will go to the Tara, where they will
sleep this night. Once they are gone, arouse the
crew softly without showing lights, and talk to
them in the forecastle, telling them what I have
said. Remember that you on the Cholita need
run no risks: only lie quietly if there are noises
from the other schooner. In the morning the Tara
will be ours and those three men our prisoners.
Seroni will see to it that no man of you is wrongly
accused. The truth is that the Government will
praise you for having refused to aid a captain who
is no better than a robber. Think of old Pahuri,
whose blood is on your decks — is that the work
of honest men?"

"Aye, and this!" A deep voice rang out as
Fatu rose from the dark corner where he had been
lying, and pointed downward with a gigantic
outstretched arm. Then for the first time I saw
Ivi, grinning at me over a shoulder done up in
blood-soaked rags. "It is well said that Rairi is
a dog," Fatu went on. "If I had my hands on

his throat once more, I would not let go so soon!"
An angry murmur went up from the divers; I perceived that the moment was ripe for my proposal.

"Who will come with me this night," I asked —
"who will follow Fatu to capture the Tara and to
set Seroni free?" Ofai sprang from his seat at Ivi's
side. The divers crowded about me eagerly to
hear my plan.

"We shall need only six or seven of the strongest," I told them. "Let us give Tua time to return
and deliver his message, and then, when Rairi
and the bearded captain have gone back to the
Tara to sleep we will swim out without noise,
climb softly on deck, and take them by surprise.
Only one man will be on watch; Seroni waits our
coming to break down the door with an axe that
will be given him."

While I lay on a mat, discussing our plan with
Maruia and the others, Tua took leave of us. I
felt a reasonable confidence that he would play
his part and keep his men from interfering on
behalf of Schmidt. Maruia's blood was up; she
was keen to go with us and it was not easy to persuade her to stay behind. An hour dragged by —
another — another — it was nearly midnight when
I gave the word to set out. Each man was naked
save for a breechclout; our bodies were well rubbed
with coconut oil, and we carried the long keen
knives used for clearing bush.

The moon had set long since, and black clouds
blotted out the stars. A stir of air from the south

caused the palms to rustle and sigh uneasily. We were in for a squall. I saw that unless the wind grew strong enough to rouse the sleepers on the Tara, the weather was in our favor: the squall would put the watcher off his guard and drown the slight noises of our approach. Presently the wind was sweeping in gusts across the lagoon, driving a fine rain into our faces. The schooner must be facing the south, with her stern toward shore.

"I think there will be a line astern," I told the men crouching beside me under the dripping hibiscus trees, "and Fatu and I will go aboard that way. You others must swim to the bow without a sound and climb up by the chain or by the jibboom stay. We will allow you time to get aboard. Wait by the forecastle till you hear the alarm given and then come aft to take them by surprise. As I told you, there will be only one man on watch, and Fatu alone can handle him. We must not use our knives unless they drive us to it. Come — it is time we set out — this squall will drown the noise of our approach."

"Yes," put in Fatu, whose closest friend was Pahuri, the old engineer, "let us go quickly! My hands yearn for the feel of Rairi's throat!"

I led the way into the water, deeper and deeper, till we were swimming in the black lagoon. We seemed an hour in reaching the Tara, anchored no more than four hundred yards offshore. The little waves slapped against my face and the rain stung my eyes. At last, when I was wondering if we had taken the wrong direction, the clouds broke and the stars shone out, disclosing the dim outlines of the Tara close ahead and Schmidt's schooner, riding at anchor a hundred yards away. At that moment a man appeared on deck, — whether Schmidt or Rairi I could not make out, — carrying a lantern in his hand. He made the lantern fast to the main boom and left it hanging there. Then he drew a deck-chair into the circle of faint light, and sat down, facing the schooner's bow.

With Fatu close behind, I swam under the overhang of the stern, and next moment my hand touched a heavy rope, trailing overboard from the rail. The half-caste girl had kept her word. The others were clustering about us, and as the wind was still strong I ventured to whisper fresh instructions there in the schooner's lee. "The rope is here," I told them softly; "do not hurry about getting aboard. Give that man time to settle down quietly in his chair. Be ready to come running aft in five minutes."

I had not reckoned on Fatu's impatience, nor on the native vagueness about time. My companion was roused as I had never seen him before. For a little while, with the greatest difficulty, I restrained his eagerness, but finally he shook my hand off his shoulder and began to pull his huge body up the rope, hand over hand. I followed: there was nothing else to do. The wind was still blowing strongly from the south.

Fatu reached the rail in an instant, heaved himself aboard with uncanny agility, and dropped to the deck without a sound. I was desperately slow in following, for I was tired and chilled, and my arms were not trained to sailors' work. When at last my head rose above the rail, I saw that the giant was stealing toward the unconscious man in the deck-chair, creeping forward with a stealthy swiftness in the shadow of the binnacle. The lantern, flickering in gusts of wind, cast a dim yellow light on the scene. Then my hand slipped on the wet rail, and I fell thumping to the deck.

I was on my feet in an instant, but the man in the chair was quicker still. It was Schmidt, and his senses must have been keen as those of a savage, for his eye was on me before I had taken a step, and the rifle came to his shoulder with a snap. In the same instant Fatu leaped at him from behind the binnacle, springing like a monstrous cat — but the spring was a breath too late. I saw a bright tongue of flame, heard a crashing report, and felt a great blow on my leg — a shock that spun my body about and sent me sprawling to the deck. I lay there sick and numb, yet keenly alive to every detail of the scene that followed: a swift drama stamped indelibly on my memory.

Fatu seized the rifle with a single mighty wrench, tore it from Schmidt's hands and sent it flying overboard, then his arms closed about the German's body. Schmidt was a very strong and active man. His foot went out behind the leg of his

antagonist; he twisted his body with the movement
of a skilled wrestler, and the pair came crashing
to the deck. But Fatu's grip never relaxed and I
knew that in the hug of those mighty arms
Schmidt's moments of consciousness were num-
bered. He seemed to realize it too, and his right
hand, free from the elbow down, began to move
painfully toward the holster at his belt, where I
saw the gleam of an ivory pistol-butt. Then I
heard my uncle's axe thundering at the stateroom
door, and the shouts of the divers, climbing over
the bows.

I raised my eyes, hoping to see the natives running aft. I glanced back at the wrestlers and saw
Raita there beside them — a slender, crouching
figure in white, her face framed in waves of dusky
hair. She had drawn Schmidt's revolver in the
nick of time, and held it cocked in her hand.

But Kwala, the black savage, who must have
been sleeping on the forward hatch, still had a
part to play. In the second while Raita crouched
there, fiercely seeking her chance to kill, there
was another streak of flame, and the report of
another rifle-shot. The girl sank down on the
deck. I saw the shock-headed savage blinking in
the lamplight while a wisp of smoke eddied from
the muzzle of his Winchester. Then, with fierce
shouts and a rush of bare feet on deck, the divers
were on him, and he went down in a smother of
brown arms and legs.

For an instant, Raita lay where she had fallen,

but though she was dying, hatred of the German gave strength for the last act of her life. "Guk!" I heard her exclaim with a weak fierceness, as her hand went out to take up the pistol a second time. By chance it had not gone off when she had dropped it. With a wavering hand she aimed it at Schmidt's temple and pulled the trigger. A third shot rang out above the tumult — Schmidt's body quivered and relaxed — Fatu rose slowly to his feet.

Out of the corner of my eye I saw a man standing at the companionway. It was Rairi, an expression of angry astonishment on his handsome, sullen face.

He glanced swiftly about him, seemed to arrive at a decision, and bounded across the deck. Before I could cry out, he was over the rail and into the lagoon.

The appearance of my uncle, dressed in a scarlet waistcloth and brandishing an axe, smothered the shout on my lips.

"Eh, Fatu!" he cried, as his eye fell on the gigantic figure of the mate. "Have you got them safe? Where's Charlie?"

"Here!" I said in a weak voice, and next moment he was bending over me. "Schmidt shot me in the leg. He's dead, I think, and so is that poor girl. Ofai and the divers have the black man — look — they're tying him now! And Rairi — he dove over the side a second before you came on deck! Quick! Send someone after him!"

At my words Fatu sprang away to lower a boat. When my uncle had made sure that Schmidt and the woman were dead and that the black was safely bound, he took me in his arms and carried me below to dress my wound. He laid me on the lounge in the saloon, turned up the lamp and bent over my wounded leg, his face wearing an expression I had never seen. Then he straightened his back with a great sigh of relief.

"Well, old fellow," he said, patting my bare shoulder, "you've given me a scare! But you're not badly hurt: the bullet has passed through the muscle of your thigh without touching the bone. Hurts like the deuce, eh? That won't last long — we'll have you on foot within a month!"

He made me drink a glass of brandy, the first I had tasted: burning stuff that made me cough and ran through my veins like fire. I was weak from loss of blood, and when he had staunched the bleeding and bandaged the wound with wet compresses, I fell into an uneasy sleep.

It was later that I was told of the happenings of that night: how one of the divers swam ashore to tell the people that Seroni was free; how a great fire was built on the beach and a fleet of canoes put off to swarm about the Tara; and how her decks were crowded with brown men and their women and children, all eager to shake my uncle's hand. It was a night of rejoicing. A fire was built in the galley to brew huge pots of tea, and cases of bully beef and ship biscuit were opened on deck.

The morning found me feverish and in pain with the stiffening of my wound. Old Maruia had installed herself in my stateroom. The season was over, she declared; she had earned enough for one year, and now she was going to nurse me till I was well. I was eating the gruel she had prepared, when I looked up and saw my uncle standing in the splintered doorway, a long cigar in his mouth.

"It's tough luck to be laid up this way!" he remarked, "Hurts, eh? It will for a few days. But you've a first-class nurse; I reckon she'll have you in a steamer-chair inside of a fortnight! I did n't know how many friends you had ashore — the whole lot of them were asking after you last night — Eh, Maruia, don't let him move that leg!

"About Rairi," he went on — "he got clean away. A Paumotu boy in the water on a dark night is a hard proposition to catch! We don't know which way he swam, of course; we'll search the two islands on the east side of the lagoon to-day. I'm leaving now; the boats will follow along the beach to the pass and meet us there to-night. With fifteen men we'll be able to comb the bush so that a dog could n't pass us! If we don't get him to-day, we'll try the west side to-morrow — You've guessed why I'm going to so much trouble? Yes, he's gotten away with your pearls!

"This morning, when the excitement was over, I made an inventory of the things in the safe. The door was open; Schmidt had left everything in place, only taking the precaution to lock the inner door. I found the key in his pocket. He never knew about the Twins — I told you how I saw Rairi steal them under his eyes. I was losing hope of coming out of this affair so well. I owe you a lot, old man; I'll try to repay part of it by getting your pearls for you. We'll catch Rairi, never fear! Schmidt and the girl were buried this morning. He was a man, that German, though he had the morals of a wolf! It's odd — but there was something I almost liked about him — It takes courage to play a game like his, and he might have succeeded if he'd been a little less contemptuous of the natives he's abused so long. I wonder who he really was! I'm sorry the girl was killed — I would have sent her home. She couldn't have been more than twenty, poor child — a forlorn way to die. The black is in irons aboard the other schooner, where he's not popular with the crew!"

When my uncle had gone I sent a man ashore for Marama, and presently he was installed in the upper berth, a mass of bandages about his swollen feet. It was good to see my friend once more.

"I do not know where Rairi is now," he said, when Maruia had left us to smoke her cigarette on deck, "but if he was barefoot when he went overboard, he will be in no shape to run away! Aué! That dry coral is sharp underfoot! When I escaped from the Cholita, I had one thought in mind; to get to Seroni quickly, to warn him and bring help to you. I landed close to the village of the copra-makers and there was an old canoe on the beach, but when I took thought, I saw that the day would break before I reached the Tara, and that I would run a risk of being picked up again by that bearded captain who is now dead, so I traveled the length of the western island afoot. The sun was high when the time came to swim, and I was faint with pain and loss of blood — the coral cuts deep! If I had been stronger I would have gone directly to the Tara, for I had no suspicion that Rairi's boat had come to her in the night. Fatu was the first man I saw on shore; he told me of the shooting, of Ivi's wound, and how Seroni was a prisoner on his own schooner. All that day I lay in great pain, and my head was light with the sun."

At midday Maruia dressed our wounds and brought up food, and we dozed through the long warm afternoon. It was evening when my uncle returned with his weary men. They had scoured the eastern islands from end to end without finding so much as a footprint.

Next day, when they searched the long island on the western side of the lagoon, the story was the same, though one of the divers claimed to have found the half obliterated tracks of a man on a stretch of muddy beach. That night my uncle went to bed with scarcely a word; I could see that he was discouraged, mystified, and very tired. Marama and I were silent for a long time after the others had gone to bed. Finally the native boy spoke.

"Are you asleep?" he asked in his own tongue. "No," I whispered back; "I lie here thinking." "And I too. Listen, for there is something in my mind. First of all, know that Rairi is not a stranger on this land of Iriatai. His mother was a woman of the island — one of the wild people the French soldiers came to take away. And when he was a boy he came here to labor at the copra-making, with the woman who lived here before Seroni's coming. There are true words! Knowing all this, I have tried to put myself in his place. He has our pearls — pearls of great value, for which a man would endure hardships and long months of waiting. The question in his mind must be: 'Where shall I hide myself till the schooners are gone and I can steal a canoe to chance a passage to the nearest land?' Where, indeed? The three islands about the lagoon are long, but they are flat and narrow. The bush is thick in places, but not too thick to be searched as one searches for a dropped fishhook in a canoe. Where, then? Listen, and I will tell you — in the Cave of the Shark! Is it not possible that in his boyhood Rairi found the cavern even as we found it, or that the woman Turia showed it to him as an ancient sacred place? He would believe that no other man on the island knew of it; that he might lie hidden there for months, stealing out by night to catch fish and to gather coconuts for food and drink. I tell you that the thought of losing our pearls has weighed like a lump of lead on my stomach, but now I feel hope!"

When my uncle had returned that evening, discouraged and empty-handed, I had felt the full
bitterness of disappointment — the hopeless col-
lapse of all my dreams. After all, our hopes had
been absurd; a three or four mile swim at night
was a risky business, even for a native. Perhaps
Rairi had been seized with cramps; perhaps a rov-
ing shark had picked him up. In reality, the chances
were against his being alive. But now, as the possi-
bility of the cave grew large in my mind, I could
scarcely wait for the morning, to tell my uncle of
Marama's idea. Eight bells struck. It was midnight, and the soft breathing in the upper berth
told me that Marama was asleep. He had a wholesome lack of nerves, and to him the loss of the
pearls meant no more than a passing disappointment. In his eyes, money was not a thing that
mattered greatly — if one had none of it, one did
without; if one's pockets were full, it was pleasant
to spend. I envied him, for with me it was far
different.

Hour after hour I lay there, wakeful with anxiety
and the fever of my wound, while the round ship's
clock in the saloon struck off the bells. The glimmer of dawn was in the stateroom when at last I
fell asleep.

Maruia woke us with a tray of breakfast, steam-
ing hot from the galley. The sun was high, and
glancing through the door, I could see my uncle,
bending over some papers at his table. My head
was heavy with lack of sleep, but the fever seemed

gone and the pain in my leg diminished. I called
to Uncle Harry and he rose at the sound of my
voice.

"Well, boys," he said, smiling in at us, with a
hand on either side of the doorway, "had a good
night? I was for letting you sleep, but the old
lady thought it was time you were eating breakfast." I told him what Marama had suggested the
night before, and his eyes lit up with a brilliant
gleam of interest.

"I believe you've hit it!" he exclaimed. "That's
the one place we haven't searched. I remember
now Schmidt's saying that, as a boy, Rairi had
lived on Iriatai. I lay awake half the night puzzling
over this business — I was beginning to believe that
the man must have been taken by a shark. But we
must waste no time; I'm off now for a look at this
cave of yours. Wish me good luck!"

The hours of that day dragged past with interminable slowness. I grew depressed as time went
on: perhaps we had been unduly sanguine the night
before; the thread supporting our hopes was a
slender one, after all. Even if Rairi were found, he
might have lost the pearls or hidden them. Marama
laughed at my fears, refusing to share in my re-
newed depression. At noon the old woman brought
us lunch and we ate with good appetites, for by
now we were on the way to recovery. Afterward,
when she had cleared the things away, I fell into
a dreamless and refreshing sleep.

It was late afternoon when I awoke. There was

a hail from the deck and the sound of a boat, bumping against the schooner's side. Next moment my uncle ran down the companionway and burst into our stateroom, a smile on his lips and in the dark brilliance of his eyes. Without a word he placed in my hands a small tin box — a box that I had seen before. I opened it with a beating heart, and there, side by side in their nest of damp cotton-wool, were the Marama Twins! The native boy, gazing down over the side of his berth, gave a shrill whoop of joy.

"It was a tame affair," remarked my uncle, when he had answered our first rapid questions, "but your cave is certainly a curious place. We had no difficulty in finding the entrance. I led the way in, with Fatu, Ofai, and a couple of others close behind. Whew! That's a bit of a swim before you can come up to blow! I had warned the men to make no noise; it was possible that Rairi might have clung to the six-shooter I had seen at his belt, and good ammunition is almost waterproof. Presently, as my eyes grew accustomed to the dim light, I made out the idol and the heathen altar, and then, on the ledge a little to one side, the huddled figure of a man. It was Rairi — his eyes were open and he had been watching us all the time. He's a plucky scoundrel; when I was standing over him wondering why he had not moved, he shook his head and grinned at me as he made an effort to hold up his right arm, blackened and horribly swollen out of shape. 'I glad you come!'

he said in a weak voice. He was burning with fever

"Then he told me what had happened. Swimming across the lagoon in the dark, he had run squarely on a patch of the purple coral, the poisonous kind that cuts like a razor-edge. He managed to get to the cave before the wounds stiffened, but next morning, when daylight began to appear through the cranny in the rock, he realized that it was all up with him unless help came. Both legs and his right arm are frightfully infected — I'm not sure that we can pull him through. Well, if he dies, it will save the Government from supporting him in jail! The pearls were in the pocket of his dungarees — he handed them to me of his own accord. We had the deuce of a time getting him out to the boat; he'd have been drowned if Fatu hadn't been along!"

XIII

TAHITI

THERE is little more to tell of our days at Iriatai.
For a fortnight, while I lay bored and convales-
cent in a steamer-chair, the diving went on. Then
each man's share of the shell was laid out for my
uncle's inspection, sacked, weighed, and loaded
in the Tara's hold. There were a hundred and
twenty tons of it, of a quality unknown in the
lagoons of the Eastern Pacific, and Uncle Harry
was jubilant over our good luck. His safe held a
little fortune in pearls, and the divers had others
they were keeping to sell on their own account.

A day came at last when the village on the islet
was dismantled; when the people crowded our
decks, noisy and gay with the joy of being home-
ward-bound; when the Tara, deeply laden, turned
her sharp bows toward the pass, away from the
anchorage which had been our home so long.

Pahuri was at his accustomed place in the engine-
room — the old man had soon recovered from
the rough handling he had endured. Ivi, with his
left arm in a sling, was the hero of the forecastle;
the divers never tired of discussing the memorable
night when he had received his wound, and I could
see that in the future the story would be passed
from island to island, growing to epic proportions
as the years went by. Marama and I had thriven

under Maruia's care; his feet were healed by now, and I was able to get about the deck, though my leg still gave me an occasional twinge.

The Cholita, with Tua in command and our two prisoners stowed away below, followed us southward toward the pass. Rairi was out of danger at last, after days of raging fever when there seemed small chance that he would live. The copra-makers had been on Iriatai for more than a year, and Schmidt's schooner halted off their village to take them aboard and load the twenty tons of copra stacked under the shed on the beach.

Outside the pass, when the Tara dipped her nose into the long Pacific swell, I lay alone on the after deck, gazing back at the line of palm-tops that was Iriatai, fast disappearing beyond the slope of the world. I thought of Schmidt, sleeping forever under a wooden cross on the deserted islet; of the woman in the shallow coral grave beside him, the half-savage girl he had stolen from her home in the far-off Carolines — Raita, who had been my friend, and whose hand, at the last, had ended his strange life. I felt a lump in my throat, as I realized that in all probability my eyes would never again rest on Iriatai, this dot of land, immeasurably lonely and remote.

A week later we dropped anchor in Faatemu Bay. The other schooner had gone on to Tahiti and would await us there. The village hummed with the excitement of our arrival; there were long stories to be told, friends and relatives to be greeted, and good fortune to be shared. Forty pigs were killed for the feast that Taura, the gray-haired chief, gave in our honor. Fat old Hina welcomed me like a mother, with easy native tears. I had not forgotten her kindness, and on the last day I tendered my parting gift: two handsome pearls — one for her, and one for my former playmate, Marama's little sister. When the Tara sailed out through the Nao Nao Passage and I went below, I found my stateroom littered with their presents — fans, hats, baskets, wreaths of bright-colored shell.

Marama and his father accompanied us to Tahiti. At dawn of the second day I was awakened by my uncle's voice, calling me on deck to see the land. The schooner was slipping through a calm gray sea, running before a light breeze from the north, and a glimmer along the horizon told of the approaching day. Close on our starboard beam, and so unreal that I half-expected the vision to fade before my eyes, I saw the fantastic pinnacles of Eimeo. Tahiti lay straight before the Tara's bows — faint, lofty outlines rising from the sea to disappear in veils of cloud. We were standing side by side at the rail, and at last my uncle spoke.

"This is my home-coming," he said quietly. "To me, that island is the most beautiful thing in all the world."

At ten o'clock we were opposite the pass, and I saw for the first time the little island port of

Papeete: the masts of trading-schooners rising along the docks; the warehouses and the line of sheds for freight; the narrow, shaded streets running inland from the waterfront; the background of green, jagged mountains, cleft by the Fautaua Gorge.

A crowd gathered while the Tara docked. There were shouted greetings in native, in English, and in French. As the schooner was warped alongside and the gangplank came out, the people began to stream aboard. The Cholita had brought news of our coming, with the story of our gold-lipped shell and Schmidt's attempted piracy. My uncle had given Tua a letter to the authorities, turning over the schooner and the prisoners to the Government, exonerating the crew, and giving a detailed account of the affair. The news had caused a stir in this peaceful and remote community; we refused a dozen invitations to lunch, and Uncle Harry was forced to tell the story twenty times — to traders, to officials, to his own agents in Papeete — before his friends would give him peace. And through it all I heard a chorus of exclamations at the gold-lipped shell.

I spent the afternoon wandering about the town. It was all new and strange to me: the strolling bands of sailors, the Chinese shops, the houses with their deep, cool verandas shaded by exotic trees. At four o'clock I met my uncle by appointment at the bank. He took me to a private room upstairs, and as he opened the door a man rose and came toward us with outstretched hand. He was small and dapper — a shade too well dressed. His nose was long, and his black eyes bright and beady as shoe-buttons; his radiant smile, under a little waxed moustache, disclosed teeth like the pearls in which he dealt.

"Monsieur Sikorsky," murmured my uncle, "my nephew, Charles."

"It is a pleasure," said the Jew, shaking my hand warmly, "to meet the nephew of my old friend. I have been aboard the Tara this afternoon and have heard much of you! They told me you had been diving with the natives — a wonderful experience, young man, but dangerous, *hein?* Ah, those sharks — those great man-eating fish — it is *épouvantable!*" He shuddered delicately, offered my uncle a cigarette from a case of tortoise-shell, and blew out a cloud of perfumed smoke.

"Yes," he went on, "Monsieur Selden has told me how old Maruia's kinsman was taken by the tonu, and how you dove down to the cave for the old oysters your native boy had seen. And he said that if I came here this afternoon you might show me the matched pearls you found that day."

"I have them here," put in my uncle, drawing the familiar tobacco-tin from his pocket. "We'll show them to Sikorsky, eh? Perhaps he'll want to make you an offer." He drew up three chairs about a table close to the window, and pulled back the blinds to admit the afternoon sunlight into the room. Then he opened the little box and laid the pearls side by side on the green tablecloth.

"Well, what do you think of them?" he asked. "You've never seen a finer matched pair, eh?"

For a moment Sikorsky lost his urbane composure. His black eyes glittered and his hand trembled a little as he reached out to take up the pearl nearest him. As he turned it over and over in his palm, admiring the perfection of its form and the play of light on its flawless surfaces, he muttered to himself in a language I had never heard. Presently he laid down the first pearl and took up the other for examination; rose to fetch a black leather case from a corner of the room; laid out his jeweler's scales and measuring instruments. Without a word to us, he weighed and measured to his satisfaction, took out writing-materials and covered a sheet of paper with the figures of a complex calculation. Then he took up the pearls for a last glance, and leaned back, lighting another of his perfumed cigarettes.

"There is no need of beating about the bush," he said. "You know pearls, Selden — such a pair does not turn up twice in a lifetime. They would make a gift for an empress! It has been a privilege to see them, even though nothing comes of it. If they were mine, I would go hungry before I would part with them!"

"What are they worth?" asked my uncle.

"Ah, that is hard to say — they are for sale?"

"Yes, at a price; I would buy them myself if I could afford to own such luxuries."

"I will make you an offer, then, though the responsibility is more than I am authorized to take. They are matched almost to the weight of a hair — Let me see — for one of them, alone, I could safely offer you twelve thousand dollars. Double that for the matching — forty eight thousand for the pair — Yes — I will make my offer fifty thousand."

He raised his hand as my uncle was about to speak.

"That is a fair offer," went on the Jew, "I assure you, a long time might elapse before my firm could find a purchaser. I would not make it except that they love fine pearls as I do. But if you think that this is not enough, name your own price and give me time to wire my people in Paris. One thing I ask of you as an old friend: show them to no one else till I have had my chance!"

"A fair enough offer, I should say," remarked my uncle, as he put the pearls in their box and rose to leave. "I must go down to the schooner now; my nephew and I will talk over your price to-night. Can you meet us here after breakfast to-morrow? We'll let you know our decision in the morning."

The pearl-buyer ushered us to the door and bowed us out with another radiant smile.

That evening, when we were sitting alone on the balcony of our hotel, Uncle Harry told me something of the Jew. "If you met Sikorsky at home," he said; "you'd think he was a little counter-jumper, but as a matter of fact there's no squarer or more decent fellow in this part of the world. I've known him for years. He speaks half a dozen languages and has been in most of the odd corners of the earth. What do you think of his offer? In your place I'd be inclined to accept. I doubt, in fact, if the Twins would fetch much more. One might take them abroad, of course, and find some rich fancier who would pay twice as much, but peddling jewels is not in our line. What do you say?"

"Oh, let's accept his offer!" I exclaimed. I had been thinking of nothing else since our visit to the bank. Half of fifty thousand dollars seemed a tremendous sum to me.

"Very well," said Uncle Harry with a smile. "To-morrow will be a great day for Marama and the old man!"

He drew from his pocket the familiar case of worn brown leather and. selected a cigar. When it was drawing to his satisfaction he tossed the match into the street and cocked his feet against the railing of the balcony.

"I've good news," he remarked. "We have a week before your steamer sails. I want you to see my place in the country. When does your school begin? The first of October? That's good — you'll be home in plenty of time. Now about the money; it's yours to do with as you like, of course, but let me give you a bit of advice. If I were you, I'd turn the bulk of it over to your father — he's in need of cash, and a few thousands would put the Santa Brigida on its feet. It will be yours eventually; stick by the land, old fellow — it doesn't pay to knock about the world as I have done. By the way, there'll be something coming to you from your lay in the season's work, though it will look small beside Sikorsky's check. Well, it's getting late — time we were turning in."

In the morning, when we had finished breakfast, we met the pearl-buyer at the bank. Half an hour later, as we shook hands and strolled out the door, I carried in the inner fold of my pocketbook a draft for twenty-five thousand dollars, on a San Francisco banking house. We found Marama and his father aboard the schooner. Their eyes were bright with wonder when my uncle told them of the bargain he had made, and they were glad to accept his offer to look after the money for them, letting them draw on him whenever they were in need of funds.

"I'm having some friends to dinner to-morrow," he told me as we walked down the gangplank. "We must be getting out to Fanatea now. My boat got in early this morning — come along and have a look at her."

She was lying a quarter of a mile down the beach, moored to the sea-wall under the old trees bordering the avenue. On her narrow stern I saw the word "Marara" lettered in gold, and her lean lines and the six great exhaust-pipes standing in a row left no doubt that she could show the speed of her namesake, the flying fish. A native in a suit of oily overalls sprang ashore to greet us and smiled when I spoke to him in his own tongue.

"What do you think of her?" asked my uncle. "Isn't she a beauty? I built her myself — every plank. That's a French engine — ninety horse-power — and it drives her at better than twenty knots!"

The mechanician fetched our bags from the hotel. We took our places in the cockpit, the spray-hood was raised, the anchor came up, and the stern line was cast off. The deep-throated roar of the exhaust brought a little crowd to the quay while the man turned up grease cups and oiled a bearing here and there. He raised his head and glanced at my uncle with the odd native lift of the eybrows which means "All ready!" The motor burst into a deeper and a fiercer roar; my uncle took the wheel and pulled back the lever of the clutch. The boat quivered and sprang forward swiftly, heading for the docks where the stevedores were dropping their wheelbarrows to watch. She swept around the harbor in a great curve, turned seaward, and headed out through the pass, her bows parting the waves in sheets of spray. Outside the reef we swung southward toward Fanatea, twenty miles off.

An hour later I saw a break in the white line of the reef. As we sped in through the gap, the huge blue combers, with spray whipping back from their crests, raced in on either side of us to topple and crash in thundering foam.

"There's Fanatea!" shouted my uncle, pointing to a long white house at the end of an avenue of palms.

A path, bordered by ornamental palms, led from the pier to my uncle's house, set on a rise of land a quarter of a mile beyond. The plantation had a long frontage on the beach and extended inland, across the rich alluvial flat, up into the hills. More than two hundred acres were planted with coconuts, — stately young palms in rows ten yards apart, — and lines of fencing divided the land into paddocks, where I saw fat cattle grazing belly-deep in grass.

The house was long and low, plastered with burned coral from the lagoon. The veranda overlooked a matchless view of dark-green foreshore, placid lagoon, white reef, and sparkling sea. Far off across the channel the horizon was broken by Eimeo's jagged peaks. Deep, cool, and airy, the veranda was my uncle's living-room, and at the windward end, in a great glassed-in bay, I found his collection of idols, weapons, and native implements. That night, when the Chinese house-boy rang the gong, I scarcely knew Uncle Harry in pumps, flannel trousers, and a smart white dinner-coat. It was his custom to potter about all day on the plantation, bush-knife in hand and clad only in a cotton pareu; but when evening came and he had had his bath, he never failed to appear immaculate at the dinner hour.

"This is the only home I have," he remarked as we sat down, "and when I'm here I make a little effort to keep up appearances. It saves me from becoming a savage. I have a good many friends scattered about the island — I visit them sometimes and they often come here. As I told you, a few of them will be out to-morrow: Sikorsky is coming and a couple of Government men. Old Jackson said he would come, too — he's my agent here; by the way, he's reserved a deck cabin for you on the steamer. Maruia is the most famous cook on the island — she's promised to come out to superintend the kitchen."

Maruia arrived early the next afternoon, and when she had shaken hands with us she went straight to the back of the house, where the Fanatea people, who stood in awe of such a rich and celebrated character, sprang this way and that to do her bidding.

The motor-boat had gone to town, and just before sunset I heard the hoarse bellow of her exhaust and saw her moving swiftly across the lagoon toward the pier. When he had presented me to his guests, my uncle took the Frenchmen in charge and left me with old Mr. Jackson and Sikorsky. The gold-lipped shell and his adventure with Schmidt had made Uncle Harry the hero of the hour, and since the Jew had showed the Marama Twins to several of his friends, I found myself an object of interest to these older men. But Mr. Jackson, a gaunt old Englishman with

friendly eyes and an enormous white moustache.
knew how to put me at my ease.

"A beautiful pair of pearls," he remarked when
we were walking into the dining-room; "they'll
make a sensation in Paris! Sikorsky showed them
to me last night; he's planning to take the next
boat north, on his way to France. Told me how
you found them, too — the tonu and all the rest
of it. Bad brutes, those tonus — one nearly had
me when I was a lad. Forty years ago, that was —
I'm getting old, eh? In those days I was super-
cargo aboard a schooner of the Maison Brander.
We were lying becalmed inside the pass at Mangareva, and in spite of what the natives said, I
thought I'd have a bit of a swim. In the nick of
time I saw the brute coming up at me — a great
spiny, mottled beast, with a mouth like an open
door. We were towing a boat, by good luck — I
went over her stern so fast I scraped half the skin
off my chest!"

"He's off!" said my uncle, at the other end of
the table. "Mr. Jackson's our champion spinner
of yarns, Charlie; he's a true artist, and you
must n't believe everything he says!"

The old man chuckled — they were friends of
many years standing. "I'll promise not to do any
more talking," he said. "I'm hungry, and I can
tell by that salad of shrimps that old Maruia is
somewhere about. Lucky man! How did you
persuade her to officiate?"

An hour later, when the Chinese boy had

brought coffee, one of the Frenchmen pushed back his chair and rose. He was the treasurer of the colony, a stout, middle-aged man, with keen dark eyes and a close-cropped beard.

"First of all," he said, with a friendly smile at my uncle, "permit me to thank you for an excellent dinner, such as I know how to appreciate. Nor must we forget Maruia, whose skill in her art I have known for so many years. And now let me propose the health of our host, whose discovery of gold-lipped shell in the Paumotus marks an addition to the resources of the colony. To Monsieur Selden, then, whose enterprise has earned the Government's warm thanks!"

My uncle rose as the Treasurer sat down. "Monsieur Durand has been more than kind," he said. "And speaking of Maruia, she has been good enough to offer to entertain us this evening. You all know the old-time native songs, and how rarely one hears them nowadays. She has composed an *uté* on our diving-season at Iriatai. I think she is waiting for us on the veranda — bring your coffee along."

We found her in the bay-window, examining a piece of tapa cloth. She seemed known to all the company and perfectly at ease, addressing Mr. Jackson in native and the others in fluent French. Her hair, which was brushed back loosely, was fastened with a pearl-studded clasp at the nape of her neck; golden earrings were in her ears, and she wore a flowing gown of thin black silk. I could scarcely believe that this was the old savage beside whom I had dived day after day, the fierce creature who had leaped overboard, spear in hand and muttering a heathen prayer, to avenge her nephew's death.

I sat down between Mr. Jackson and Sikorsky, on a long lounge covered with a scarlet-bordered mat. Beyond the railing of the veranda a score of natives squatted on the grass.

Maruia took her place cross-legged on the floor, and a boy placed in her hands a great piano-accordion, inlaid with mother-of-pearl. In the silence which proved the interest of her audience, she drew out the bellows and let her fingers play over the stops. Then I heard for the first time the music of the uté — a wild minor melody, stirring, exultant, heathen, and profoundly sad. Suddenly she began to sing, in a high-pitched wail, a song such as our ancestors must have sung in the firelight, centuries before history dawned. Here and there I could catch a word, — enough to piece together the story the verses told, — but the language was full of imagery and many of the words were of the ancient tongue which only a few of the older people understood. She sang of how the Tara came to Faatemu and sailed away to Iriatai; of how Seroni killed the old god in the form of a shark; and of the temple in the cave; of the strange shell with lips like gold, such as no man in the Paumotus had seen; of her nephew's death, and how Teura had been avenged; of Schmidt and the fight aboard the schooner, when the woman from a far land was killed.

All this sounds commonplace enough, as I read over the words I have set down, but there was something far from commonplace in the quality of the woman's voice, in the wild imagery of her words, in the primitive and stirring cadences of her song. At last the music died away, and Maruia leaned back with a sigh as she snapped the hooks of her accordion.

We were silent for a time, and then my uncle spoke. He turned to Mr. Jackson.

"It's curious," he observed — "the spell of those old songs!" The trader looked up at him, raising his snowy eyebrows in the native gesture of assent.

"Either there's real art in a thing of that kind," he answered, "or I've become a savage after forty years!"

The Jew had not moved once while Maruia sang. The perfumed cigarette, forgotten between his fingers, had burned out. The old man's words seemed to rouse him from a reverie.

"Ah, gentlemen," he said, more seriously than I had heard him speak before, "make no mistake — the essence of all art is in such a song! So our old Hebrew minstrels sang, long before my people's captivity in Egypt! So, perhaps, the Greek bards sang of the fall of Troy!"

As the next day was Sunday, we persuaded our guests to stop over, and it was late afternoon when we took our places in the motor-boat, slipped out through the pass, and headed north along the reef. The breeze had died away and the Marara drove through a long, gentle swell, running in from the west. I was beginning to understand my uncle's love of the island: on such an evening, it was impossible to believe that any part of the world could be more beautiful. Beyond the line of breakers the lagoon lay like a mirror in the sunset calm, and I saw the smiling coastal land, with its coconut and breadfruit groves, sheltered at the mouths of valleys which pierced the lofty wooded hills. Out to the west, half hidden in clouds all rosy and edged with gold, Eimeo rose from unruffled waters. A long spit of land ran out to sea ahead of us.

"Point Venus," remarked my uncle, leaning over to speak in my ear. "The speck of white at the end is the lighthouse, the only one in this part of the world. It is built on the site of Captain Cook's observatory; he came here, you know, to observe the transit of Venus in 1769. He was a wonderful man —have you read the account of his voyages? Ah, you've a treat ahead! His ship anchored in Matavai Bay, this side of the point, and he named the group the Society Islands, in honor of the Royal Society, which sent him out. Sometimes I wish I could have lived in those days, when there were still islands left to discover — "

We were turning into the pass. Half an hour later we had bidden our guests good-night, and the Marara was speeding homeward in the dusk.

My week at Fanatea passed with the swiftness

of a dream, and the day came all too soon when I said good-bye to the people of the plantation and stepped aboard the boat for the last time. As we entered the pass at Papeete, I saw the mail steamer from New Zealand lying alongside the dock, hideous and huge beside the trim sailing vessels of the port. She was to carry me to San Francisco.

We went aboard at once to look up my stateroom and inquire at what hour the steamer would sail. The captain, a gray-haired Englishman, with a red face and a great jutting stomach, tightly buttoned in a double-breasted coat of drill, was an old friend of my uncle's. He called us to his quarters by the bridge.

"Hello, Selden," he said, "they tell me you've had a row with old Thursday Island. He was done in, eh? Good job, to my way of thinking! An odd bloke; gentleman born, I should say, but a hard case, and crook as they make 'em! I knew him out in the Solomons, in ninety-eight." He turned to me, holding out an enormous hairy hand.

"I've heard about you, young man," he rumbled. "You're the lad who found Sikorsky's pearls, eh? He's going north with us. They're aboard now, safe in the purser's strongbox. I'll tell the chief steward to put you at my table. We'll be sailing by three o'clock."

We lunched aboard the Tara that day, and when the meal was finished my uncle and I sat talking in steamer-chairs on deck. "It's hard to see you go, old fellow," he said. "I'll be lonely without you;

but don't forget that you're coming down again.
I wish I could go north with you now — I'd give
something to be there when your father hears of
our good luck, and sees how tall and strong you've
grown! But I'll be up next year without fail; perhaps I'll bring the Tara, and you'll see Marama
and the rest of them again. I've always wanted a
cruise down the Lower Californian coast, to have
a look at those Mexican islands and bays. Give
my love to your father and mother, and to Marion
— tell them how glad I am that they let you come
with me. This is for your sister, by the way; take
good care of it — perhaps you'd better put it in
the purser's safe." He handed me a little plush-
lined jewel-case, opening it to display a string of
beautifully graduated pearls.

"I've been collecting them for several years,"
he went on with a smile. "Marion is the only niece
I have, and I hope this will give her pleasure for a
long time to come. But it's time you were getting
aboard — the men are up forward, waiting for you
to say good-bye."

I felt a lump in my throat as I shook hands with
them, one after the other: Ofai, Ivi with his bandaged arm, Pahuri, Fatu, and the cook. Marama
and the chief of Faatemu were standing with
Maruia on the dock.

"My heart is heavy to-day," said Marama, as I
took his hand, "but Seroni has promised that I
shall go with him when next he sails away to your
land. Perhaps it will not be long before we meet."

"Come back to us one day," said the old woman. "Your welcome will be warm, for your friends are many in these islands!"

"*E, parau mau,*" put in Taura, in his deep voice. "Those are true words!"

The ship was whistling for the last time. Half laughing and half vexed at the delay, my uncle seized my arm to drag me away from the group of kind native friends. As we pushed our way through the crowd about the gangplank, the sailors were casting off the lashings. Uncle Harry grasped my hand.

"Time you were aboard," he said. "Good-bye, old man."

The gangplank came up, lines were cast off, and the propeller began to churn. I stood by the rail, gazing down at the faces of friends among the crowd ashore, while the steamer backed, turned, and headed for the open sea. A handkerchief fluttered on the Tara's deck; her ensign dipped gracefully in a farewell salute. All at once a feeling of sadness came over me — I turned my eyes away from the land, walked blindly to my stateroom, and closed the door.

That evening, when the bugle announced the dinner hour, I went on deck and gazed back across the calm sea astern. The far-away peaks of Tahiti and Eimeo stood like faint blue clouds on the line where sea met sky — lands of enchanted memory, fast disappearing in the fading light.